Tales from China's Classic Essential Readings
中国蒙学经典故事丛书

Tales from the Thousand Character Classic

《千字文》故事

姜晓东 *Jiang Xiaodong*◎著
[美]艾梅霞 *Martha Avery*◎译

CHINA INTERCONTINENTAL PRESS
五洲传播出版社

前言

中国古代重视对儿童和青少年的教育，产生了多种流传很广的启蒙读物，以使学生加强修养，增长智慧。《三字经》《百家姓》《千字文》和《幼学琼林》就是这些蒙学读物中的佼佼者，它们的主要功能是使学生认识汉字，并对他们进行文化和品德教育。

这些蒙学读物内容通俗易懂，形式简单，读起来很像歌谣，非常适合读者朗读和背诵。对很多中国人来说，这些读物是对他们一生影响最大的书籍，他们通过这些读物认识汉字，了解中国的历史、地理、社会等多方面的知识，并受到品德教育。直到今天，中国人仍然喜爱和重视这些蒙学读物。

上面提到的四本书中，《千字文》产生最早，是南北朝时梁朝人编写的，4个字一句，共250句，1000个字，所以称为“千字文”。

《三字经》产生于宋代，并经过后人的修改。它每句3个字，所以叫“三字经”。全书总共约500句，其中讲的许多观念和道理，对中国人影响深远。《三字经》已经被联合国教科文组织选入儿童道德修养的必读书目，译成多国文字，在全世界范围内发行。

《百家姓》也产生于宋代，是有关中国人姓氏的启蒙读物，采用4个字一句的歌谣形式，共计568字，介绍了504个中国人的姓氏。

《幼学琼林》在这四本书里产生最晚，是明朝人编写的。它内容极为丰富，几乎是一部小型的自然和社会百科全书，所以有人说“读了《幼学》走天下”。

这些书中蕴藏着丰厚的中华民族历史文化传统，尤其是其中提到的那些隽永、生动的故事，令读者印象深刻。“中国蒙学经典故事”丛书从上述四本书中精选出一些在中国广泛流传的故事，以简短而生动有趣的文字讲述出来，通过它们，向全世界广大的读者介绍中华民族的历史文化知识和思想、道德观念。书中的故事分成若干现代人容易理解的类型，并配以幽默生动的漫画。

这套丛书不仅适合儿童和青少年，也适合广大对中国文化感兴趣、初步接触中国历史文化的读者。

Preface

The ancient China long ago has stressed on the child and youth education. Many primer readings spreading far and beyond came into focus, thus strengthening the cause of child upbringing and brightness. *The Three Character Classic, the Hundreds Surnames, the Thousand Character Classic, and the Children's Knowledge Treasury* are the best examples of such primer readings. Their main goal is to enable the child to learn characters and educate them about culture and morality.

The readings are easy to understand, and simple to read and recite as they resemble songs. They influenced the lives of many Chinese. They learned Chinese, as well as gaining knowledge on Chinese history, geography, and society. They are well-educated on morality too. Till today, Chinese still love and stress these readings.

Of the above-mentioned four books, *the Thousand Character Classic* came out earliest. It was compiled by a man of the Liang Dynasty. With four characters in each sentence, there are 250 sentences and 1,000 characters in the book. Due to this reason, the book is titled *the Thousand Character Classic*.

The Three Character Classic came out during the Song Dynasty times and was modified later. As it has three characters in each sentence, the book is titled the Three Character Classic. It comprises about 500 sentences. Many ideas and truths in it have profound impact on the Chinese people. UNESCO incorporated the book into a list of compulsory books dedicated for the child moral education. It was translated into many languages and circulated globally.

The Hundreds Surnames came out during the Song Dynasty times. It is a primer reading related to the Chinese surnames. With a total of 568 characters and in the form of songs with four characters in each sentence, it introduced 504 Chinese surnames in all.

The Children's Knowledge Treasury came out the latest. The people of Ming Dynasty compiled this book. With rich contents, it became a mini-encyclopeadia of natural and social sciences. It owns the reputation of "Making you knowledgeable enough after reading *the Children's Knowledge Treasury*".

We can see profound historical and cultural traditions clearly in these books - especially those vivid and meaningful tales greatly impress the readers. *Tales from China's Classic Essential Readings* has selected tales spreading far and beyond in China from the above four books and tells them in short, lively and interesting truths. Readers, around the world, can learn the historical and cultural knowledge of the Chinese nation, ideology and morality through them. The tales are divided into categories to be easily understood by modern people, with the support of humorous and vivid cartoons.

The books are not only suitable for children and youth, but also for readers with interest in Chinese culture. They can experience the contact with Chinese history and culture.

Contents
目录

传说故事
Legendary Tales

历史故事
Historical Tales

美德故事
Tales of virtue

人才故事

Tales of Talents

Legendary Tales
传说故事

仓颉造字

原文：

shǐ zhì wén zì
始 制 文 字

故事：

相传在远古的黄帝时代，人们有很多发明创造，他们开始造房子、缝制衣服、制造车子和船、使用弓箭，等等，生活质量大大提高，进入了文明时代。而这个时代很重要的一件事，是创造了文字。据说，汉字是由仓颉（jié）创造出来的。

仓颉是黄帝的一个部下，他的相貌很奇特，脸上长着四只眼睛（也有人说是六只）。黄帝让他负责管理部落里一些重要的事，比如牲畜的数目、食物的数量、祭祀活动的时间、人口的增减，等等。开始的时候，仓颉采用以前的人们流传下来的办法，叫“结绳记事”，在绳子上打结来记录各种事情的变化，用不同颜色的绳子表示不同的事，用绳结的数目表示牲畜、食物等的数量。可是时间长了，事情的变化

越来越复杂，打的绳结就显得不够用了，有时会发生错误。

怎么办呢？仓颉是个很聪明的人，他想到了用刀子在竹子或木头上刻记号，取代了打绳结的方法。但是，用刀子在竹子和木头上刻画牲畜、食物的形状，需要花很长时间。为了寻找一种简便的记录方法，仓颉苦思冥想。

有一天，他跟部落里的人一起去打猎，在地上看到各种动物留下的脚印。各种动物的脚印各不相同，有经验的猎人就一一指出，哪个是鹿留下的，哪个是羊留下的，哪个又是老虎留下的。仓颉忽然受到启发：为什么不用脚印这样的简单符号来代表一种动物呢？同样的道理，其他的事物也可以用简单的符号来代表呀！他高兴极了，马上开始研究能够代表各种事物的符号。他仔细观察身边各种事物，观看太阳、月亮、星辰的形状，远望大地山川起伏的形状，还留意乌龟背上上的花纹、小鸟留下的足迹，等等，给各种飞禽走兽和身边的事物都找到了合适的符号。这时候人类开始进入文明时代，新鲜事物越来越多，事情变得很繁杂，仓颉尝试将已经造好的符号组合起来表示复杂的事物。这样，就形成了早期的汉字。

仓颉试着用他造出来的文字记录自己的工作，效果非常好，每件事情都管理得又快又准确。黄帝对仓颉的工作成果很满意，向他仔细了解他的发明创造。仓颉把他造的字献给黄帝，黄帝大加赞赏，让他把这些文字及其使用方法传授给其他人。渐渐地，大家都开始使用文字了。

仓颉发明文字，贡献很大，黄帝就任命他为史官，专门记录历史。

人类发明了文字这件事传到天上，天神知道人类将很快了解大自然的秘密，于是，他就从空中像下雨一样降下各种谷物，提醒人类不要只顾着高兴，还是要注意粮食生产，以免将来挨饿。而鬼怪们听说这件事后，担心人类用文字记录下他们的样子和罪行，它们再也无法躲藏，于是一个个害怕得哭起来。安静的夜晚，到处传来鬼怪们的哭声。

汉字当然不可能是仓颉一个人创造出来的，仓颉造字的传说，表达了人们对创造出文字的先民的尊敬。

Cang Jie Creates the Chinese Script

Tradition holds that people created many new things in the days of ancient emperor Huang Di, such as how to build houses, how to sew clothes, how to make carts and boats, use bows and arrows, and so on. Life was greatly improved by these things and people entered what could be called a civilized era. In this era, one of the most important creations was scripts. It is said that Chinese "characters" were created in these early days by a person named Cang Jie.

Cang Jie was a subordinate of the Huang Di and his appearance was rather unusual. He had four eyes on his face, although some say he had six. The Huang Di had him do various important tasks in managing his realm, such as count the number of livestock, the amount of grain, keep track of when to conduct rituals and of increases and decreases in his number of people. At the beginning, Cang Jie kept track of these things by using a method people had used forever, namely tying knots in a string. Different colors of string were used for different categories of things being counted, and the knots indicated how many of each thing there were. As time went on, however, this system became more and more complex as the numbers of things multiplied.

Indeed, at times mistakes were made.

Being an intelligent man, Cang Jie thought up a new method of scribing marks on a piece of wood or bamboo with a knife. This was an improvement over the old string method, but it still took a long time. Cang Jie began to contemplate how to create a simpler method of recording things.

One day, he was out hunting with a fellow tribesman and he noticed tracks on the ground left recently by different animals. He no-

ticed that each animal had its unique footprint and that experienced hunters could tell you exactly what had passed by, a deer came here, an ibex went there, here is where the tiger came through, and so on. Suddenly inspired, Cang Jie thought to himself, why not use a symbol such as these hoof prints and paw prints to indicate the type of animal he was counting? Using the same logic, he could also use symbols to represent other things! Ecstatic at the realization, he immediately began to think up symbols for all the various things he needed to record. He examined all things around him closely, he observed the shapes of the sun, the moon, the stars, the way that mountains in the distance rose and fell on the horizon, he observed the patterns on the backs of tortoises, the tracks of little birds, and so on. For each kind of living thing and for all the things around him, he created appropriate symbols. Mankind began to use "writing" to "elucidate" things, and the combination of those two words in Chinese forms the Chinese word for "civilization." Mankind began an era of civilization. As new things multiplied in quantity and became more complicated, Cang Jie experimented with combining his various symbols to express more complex matters. In this fashion, he formed the early shapes of "Han characters" or the Chinese script.

Cang Jie also experimented with using the new script to record his own work, with excellent results. He could manage things more quickly and accurately. The Huang Di was pleased with Cang Jie, who gave the invention to him and explained its concepts in detail. The Huang Di disseminated this new practice of using a script to record things throughout the land, so that others could use the script too. In time, everyone began to use it.

Since Cang Jie's contribution in creating a script was so important, the Huang Di made him an official, in charge of recording history.

News of the invention of scripts by mankind made its way up to the heavens, where heavenly beings realized that humans would quickly be able to understand the secrets of nature now that they had invented this tool. Therefore, like rain, they sent down all kinds of grains to the earth, to remind man that he should not just run around being happy but should also concentrate on producing food in order to avoid being hungry in the future. Once ghosts and demons also heard about this invention, they were afraid that humans would use scripts to record their appearance and their bad deeds and they were afraid that they would no longer be able to hide. As a result, they began to cry. On quiet evenings, you can still hear their strange calls.

Naturally, the Chinese script was not created by one man alone. The legend of how Cang Jie created Chinese characters is meant to express the respect that we humans have for our forebears in creating a system of writing.

嫘祖养蚕制衣

原文：

nǎi fú yī shang
乃服衣裳

故事：

相传黄帝时代的人们还发明了养蚕、编织丝绸、缝制衣服的方法，而这些工作，是在黄帝的妻子嫘（léi）祖的带领下完成的。

在黄帝庆祝战胜蚩（chī）尤的盛大聚会上，来了许多嘉宾，其中一位是少女变成的女蚕神，她向黄帝献上了一束洁白光亮的细丝。当时人们已经懂得加工动物的皮毛、树皮里的纤维等来制作衣服，但蚕丝这么美丽的材料，人们还是第一次见到。聪明能干的嫘祖拿到这蚕丝之后，很快以她灵巧的双手织成一块又轻又软的绢，用它给黄帝做了漂亮的礼服和礼帽。

当时，嫘祖带领一些人，负责为部落里的人们制作衣服，有人负责做帽子，有人负责做衣服，有人负责做鞋子。为了获得做衣服的材料，嫘祖带着人每天辛苦地剥树皮、纺麻网、加工动物皮毛。

见到蚕丝之后，嫘祖觉得这是很好的衣料，可是女蚕神所吐的丝是有限的，怎样才能源源不断地获得蚕丝呢？她向蚕神详细了解蚕的习性和蚕丝的来历，知道蚕喜欢吃一种叫桑树的叶子，于是决定找到这种树，以便人工养蚕。

嫘祖带领部落里的女性到处寻找，一种树一种树地辨别。工夫不负有心人，她们终于发现一片桑树林，远看去，树上好像结满了雪白的果实。嫘祖观察发现，那雪白的果实其实是蠕动的蚕虫口中吐出的细丝绕织而成的圆壳，叫作“茧”。她把茧带回去，把它们放在水里煮，然后把木棍伸进去搅拌，结果抽出了一根根像头发那样细的白丝线。

在嫘祖的建议下，黄帝下令让人民大量种植桑树，为蚕提供了源源不断的叶子。而嫘祖自己则开始亲自养蚕。经过

很多次尝试，她终于掌握了养蚕、获得蚕茧、将蚕茧加工成丝线的一整套方法。这些经她之手生产出的丝线，与女蚕神所献的丝一样美丽光洁。嫘祖非常高兴，带领妇女们整天忙着抽丝、织出丝绸，然后为大家裁制漂亮的衣服。从此，养蚕、织布成为中国女性最主要的工作，而男性则负责狩猎和耕种粮食。

有了合适的衣料，嫘祖又开始研究如何更好地利用它们。她认为，应该将上衣和下身穿的衣服区分开来；另外，身份地位不同的人，应该穿不同的衣服，这样就可以很容易地将他们区分开来。

此后，嫘祖为推广蚕桑事业，教更多的人学会养蚕、治丝、织绢，到处奔走忙碌，最终病逝在路上。作为最早的养蚕人，她受到后世人们的尊敬，成为养蚕行业崇拜的女神。在古代，每年春天，中国皇帝都要模仿神农举行耕种仪式，而皇后则模仿嫘祖举行养蚕仪式。

由于嫘祖等人的发明创造，古代中国被称为丝绸之国。有了丝绸，才有了后来闻名世界、影响深远的“丝绸之路”。

Lei Zu Raises Silkworms and Weaves Cloth

Legend has it that other inventions were made by humans during the era of Huang Di, such as how to weave silk into fabrics and sew the fabric into clothing. People say that these things were accomplished under the leadership of Huang Di's wife, Lei Zu, or Ancestress Lei.

When Huang Di held a victory celebration commemorating his triumph over Chi You, among the many guests was a young woman who was actually the goddess of silk, transformed into a human for the occasion. She made an offering to Huang Di of lustrous pure-white silk threads. At time, people already knew how to process animal skins into hides, and how to make useful fibers out of tree bark, but this beautiful material called silk was something new. The moment Lei Zu got hold of it, she began to weave it with her nimble hands into a piece of soft and light juen, which is a particular kind of silk fabric. She then used it to make a handsome set of ceremonial robes and a ceremonial hat for Huang Di.

At the time, Lei Zu was in charge of a group of people in the tribe who were charged with making clothes for people. Some were responsible for hats, some for clothes, some for shoes. They spent tremendous amounts of time processing the materials for these things, scraping bark off trees, weaving hemp into nets, processing animal hides. All of this was hard work.

After seeing the silk of the silkworms, Lei Zu realized that this would be a marvelous material for clothing. The silk that the goddess of silk had 'spit out' at the celebration was limited, however, so the question became how to find a continuous source of the raw silk. After asking the goddess in detail about how silkworms operate and where the silk comes from, she found out that silkworms must eat a particular

kind of leaf that grows on the mulberry tree. She determined that she would find this tree so that people could raise their own silkworms.

She led the women in the tribe throughout the land, searching among all the trees, differentiating one from another and trying to locate mulberry trees. Work does not deter anyone who is determined, and in the end Lei Zu found a mulberry forest. Seen from afar, it appeared to be covered with white fruit. Looking at the fruit more closely, Lei Zu saw that this was in fact little white cases of silk. Each round encasement was being spit out by a wriggling silkworm that was hidden inside, and the encasements came to be called cocoons. Lei Zu took these cocoons home and boiled them in water, then used a stick to stir them so that the filaments adhered to the stick. Drawing these out, she found that she had fine white silken threads, like very soft hair.

At Lei Zu's recommendation, Huang Di sent forth an edict that required people to plant a large number of mulberry trees, in order to provide an unending source of food for the silkworms. Lei Zu herself began to raise silkworms. After much experimentation, she finally learned how to do it properly and was able to raise silk as lustrous and beautiful as that offered to the emperor by the goddess of silk. Happy as she could be, Lei Zu now spent her days drawing silk from cocoons, then weaving silk with the other women, then sewing it into beautiful clothing. From this point on, raising and weaving silk became the primary occupation of women in China, while men were responsible for hunting and tilling the fields for grain.

Now that she had suitable material, Lei Zu began to research how better to use it. She felt that it would be good to distinguish clothing worn on the upper part of the body from that worn on the lower part, and also to use clothing to differentiate among different kinds of people. In this way, it would be easier to see at a glance who was who, by seeing what they wore.

After this, Lei Zu began to travel widely in promoting the silk industry, teaching more people how to raise silkworms, process the silk, and weave fabric, until and in the end she became ill and died along the way. As the first one to raise silkworms, she is revered by later generations and has herself become a venerated goddess in the silk industry. In olden times, every spring the emperor would perform a ceremony that ritually enacted the planting of grain by the god of agriculture, Shen Nong. The empress in turn ritually enacted the raising of silkworms as first done by Lei Zu.

Due to the inventions of people like Lei Zu, in ancient times, China was described as the country of silk. Given its silk, in later times it came to be at the end of the famous trade route known as the "Silk Road."

大禹治水

原文：

jiǔ zhōu yǔ jì
九州禹迹

故事：

传说在上古尧帝、舜帝的时代，水神共工为了表达对天帝的怨恨，让黄河等大河的河水倒流，引发了一场旷日持久的大洪水。这下子，生活在大地上的人们随时面临水灾的威胁，没有地方居住，处境非常危险。

尧帝派鲧（gǔn）去治水。鲧带领人们修建了许多堤坝，但这些堤坝根本无法阻挡洪水泛滥，治了很多年，鲧的努力都失败了。他到天庭偷了一种叫息壤的神奇之土，只要把一小块息壤投进汹涌的洪水中，它就能不断地生长，越来越大，越来越高，把洪水堵住。但天帝发现这件事后，非常生气，派人杀死了鲧，并把息壤收了回去。结果洪水又开始到处为害。

舜帝登基后，委派鲧的儿子大禹继续治水。这时天帝也改变主意，愿意把息壤送给大禹，以帮助他治水。

大禹首先率领众神灵前去与水神共工战斗，将他驱逐到远方，以断绝水患的根源。然后，大禹把息壤撒到洪水之中，水中很快出现了一块块陆地，有些地方甚至形成了高山。人民暂时有了安身的地方，可是大地上的河道依然不畅通。大禹从父亲治水的悲剧中了解到，只依靠围堵的方法，是不能成功的。他改变思路，决定带领人们开挖河道，让洪水流到大海里去，这样才能彻底解决洪水灾害。

他首先带人去治理北方的黄河。黄河是古代中国人心目中最大、最重要的河流。黄河从发源地流出之后，经过一片原

野，来到龙门山，古时候龙门山和其他的山连在一起，完全挡住了黄河的河道，形成一片汪洋。大禹决定凿断龙门山，为河水开出一条通道。山石非常坚硬，难以凿开，但他毫不退缩，每天凿山不止。在他的带动下，人民齐心协力，终于将山凿通了。滔滔黄河水冲过了龙门山，被凿断的龙门山就像两扇大门。传说每年黄河里的鲤鱼都要逆流而上，来到这里，能够跳跃通过这段河道的，就变成拥有无穷威力的龙。

河水冲出龙门山，进入今天的河南省之后，又遭到另一座名叫砥柱山的大山的阻挡。大禹率领人们在砥柱山上凿开三个缺口，使黄河通过，这就是现在的三门峡。这样一来，黄河就可以一路奔流，浩浩荡荡地进入东海。

治理完黄河，大禹又奔走于中国各地，继续治理其他河流，包括另一条水灾严重的大河淮河。他忙着治水，很晚才结婚，而且新婚不久就离开家，继续治水。在治水的过程中，他非常勤奋和敬业，多次经过家门，居然都没有来得及进去看望妻子和儿子。

经过十多年的努力，大禹终于成功治理了中国所有的河流。长期繁重而艰苦的工作，使这位治水英雄的身体受到很大损害，他的身体极其消瘦，双手的指甲都没有了，小腿上的汗毛全部脱落，腿脚都变了形，走路也变得困难。

治水完毕，大禹受到人民的拥戴，最后，他从舜帝那儿继承了帝王之位。

Great Yu Tames the Waters

According to legend, back in the days of Yao and Shun, in order to express his displeasure with the god of heaven, the god of water, Gong Gong, made the rivers flow backwards. This caused huge and unending floods. People who lived on earth were subject to disaster at any time. There was no safe place to live, and the situation was extremely dangerous.

Yao therefore dispatched Gun to tame the waters. Gun organized the building of dikes, but these were essentially useless against the raging waters of a flood and, after a few years, Gun had simply failed. He then went up to heaven and stole a magical kind of earth. All he had to do was throw it in the torrent and the earth would grow, and grow, and eventually dam up the flood. The god of heaven was furious when he learned about this. He had Gun killed and he retrieved his magical earth, with the result that floods raged once again.

Once Shun ascended the throne, he dispatched Gun's son, Yu, to tame the waters. By this time, the god of heaven had changed his mind about the use of "earth," and he now allowed the Great Yu to use it in controlling floods.

At first, the Great Yu led troops to do battle with the god of water. He chased the god of water off into distant regions in order to get rid of the source of all the trouble. Then the Great Yu sprinkled the magical earth into the waters, whereupon earth appeared and some places even rose up into mountains. For a short time, people had a safe place to live. Rivers did not yet pass through the landscape, however. From the tragic fate of his father, the Great Yu knew that blocking up water was not reliable and would never succeed in the end. He changed his way of thinking, therefore, and decided to lead people in carving out channels through which the water could run freely. Floodwaters could safely empty out into the ocean. This way of doing things fully resolved the disastrous problem of flooding.

The Great Yu first led people in controlling the waters of the Yellow River in the north. In the minds of ancient Chinese people, the Yellow River was the greatest and most important of all rivers. After leaving its source, the river flowed across virgin lands until it reached Long-Men Mountain, "Loong-Gate Mountain." In olden days, this mountain was linked to other mountains which completely stopped up the passage of the river and made it form a marshy sea. The Great Yu decided to cut through these mountains in order to allow the water to flow out. The mountain's rocks were extremely hard and tough to cut through, but without slacking in his resolve the Great Yu kept at it every day. Under his leadership, people united in their efforts and finally were able to cut a way through. The raging waters of the Yellow River coursed through Loong-Gate Mountain, dividing the original mountain in half, like the two halves of a massive gate. It is said that the carp of the Yellow River swim back up against the current every year. When they get to this place, if they can make it through the channel, they become invincible loongs.

After the river's waters flowed through Loong-Gate Mountain, and entered what is now Henan Province, they encountered the obstruction of another great mountain called Di Zhu Mountain, or Whetstone Mountain. The Great Yu led people in cutting three gaps through this mountain, allowing the river to flow through what is now called Sanmenxia, or the Three Gorges. In this manner, the Yellow River was allowed to run freely along its entire length

and, finally, flow mightily into the eastern sea.

After taming the waters of the Yellow River, the Great Yu went throughout China taming other rivers, including one with particularly bad floods, the Huai River. Too busy taming rivers, he only married later in life and even then, shortly after the wedding, set off again. In the course of taming rivers, he had to pass by his gate many times, but had no time even to go inside and see his wife and son.

After ten years of hard work, the Great Yu succeeded in taming all of China's rivers. The pressures and hardships of the work had done great harm to this water-taming hero's body, which was now extremely weak. His fingernails were gone, the hair on his calves had fallen out, and his feet had changed shape which now made walking difficult.

After taming of the waters, the Great Yu was honored by the support and acclaim of all the people. In the end, he became next in the succession after Yao and Shun, as "Di," the Supreme Being, the monarch of the land.

任公子钓大鱼

原文：

jūn qiǎo rén diào
钧巧任钓

故事：

生活在战国时期（前475—前221）的庄子，是中国古代伟大的哲学家、思想家，道家学派的代表人物。他喜欢逍遥自在的隐居生活。他和他的学生所写的文章收集在《庄子》一书中。这本书充满神奇的想象和机智幽默的议论，讲了许多有意思的寓言故事，任公子钓大鱼的故事，就是其中一个。

任是古代的一个国家，任公子就是这个国家的一位王子。他喜欢钓鱼，可是他钓鱼的方法与普通人很不一样。一般人都拿着一根细细的钓鱼竿，守在小河或小水沟边，等着几条小鱼上钩。而任公子的钓鱼工具大得惊人，钩子巨大，钓绳又粗又长。这套钓鱼工具大到什么程度呢？鱼钩上的鱼饵竟然是五十头肥壮的牛！可想而知，任公子要钓的是一条多么大的鱼。

他坐在会（kuài）稽山（在现在的浙江省）的高处，把钓竿投到东海里面，每天都守在这里，等着他期待的大鱼。可想而知，没有什么鱼吞得下那巨大的鱼饵，所以等了整整一年，他什么也没钓上来。那些每天拿着细细的钓鱼竿去小河边钓鱼的人，却总能钓到几条小鱼，他们都不理解任公子的做法，并嘲笑他。但任公子根本不理他们，仍然专心等鱼上钩。

终于有一天，令人激动的时刻到来了：真的有一条巨大

无比的鱼吞食了那五十头牛做成的鱼饵！它拉扯着那个巨大的钓钩，快速潜没到海底深处，到处乱窜。为了挣脱钓钩，这条大鱼又冲出水面，扬起鱼鳍，摆动尾巴。它掀起的白色波浪像一座座山峰，海水剧烈地动荡，发出的声响猛烈而可怕，如同鬼神在大声哭喊，远在千里之外的人都能感觉到这种可怕的力量。那些平时嘲笑任公子的人，这时都吓得躲藏起来，看都不敢看。而任公子毫不畏惧，紧紧地握住粗大结实的钓竿，将大鱼牢牢钩住。经过一番惊心动魄的较量，那条大鱼终于死掉，被任公子拉上了岸。

任公子实现了自己的心愿，钓上了这条大鱼。这条鱼到底有多大呢？任公子将它的肉切下来，腌制成鱼干，慷慨地分给所有人。从浙江（在现在的浙江省）以东，到九嶷（yí）山（在现在的湖南省）以北，这一片非常广大地区的人们，都分到了足够的鱼肉，吃得饱饱的。

后来，那些曾经嘲笑过任公子的人，又纷纷以知情者的身份,到处向人们夸耀任公子钓大鱼的情景，仿佛他们也亲自参加了似的。但事实是，他们仍然每天拿着小钓竿，守在水沟旁守着小鱼上钩。《庄子》讲到这里，讽刺地说，像这种人，恐怕很难钓到什么大鱼吧。

《庄子》中讲完这个故事，又议论说，治理国家大事，就好像任公子钓大鱼一样，需要远大的理想和强大的力量；那些没听说过任公子钓鱼方式的人，其能力恐怕也远远不足以治理国家。

Prince Ren Catches a Great Fish

Zhuang-zi, who lived during the Warring States period (475–221 BCE), was a great philosopher and thinker and one of the key figures in the school of Daoism. He enjoyed living a carefree life as a hermit. Compositions that he and his students wrote on various subjects were later compiled into a book that is known as *Zhuang-zi*. Full of humorous anecdotes and fantastic imaginative episodes, this book narrates many fables, one of which is the story about Prince Ren catching a great fish.

Ren was a state in ancient days, and Prince Ren was one of the princes of that state. He loved to fish, but his methods were different from those of most people. Generally people fish with a long narrow rod, angling along creeks and streams, trying to catch little fish on their hooks. Prince Ren's fishing pole was so astonishingly huge, his hook so mighty, his line so thick, that the bait on the end of the hook was actually fifty sturdy cows! One can imagine the size of the fish that Prince Ren intended to catch.

He sat on the heights of Kuai-ji Mountain (in today's Zhejiang Province), and put his line into the Eastern Sea. He sat there every day, just waiting to catch his big fish. As can be imagined, no fish could swallow that enormous bait and so he sat there for a full year, not getting so much as a bite. Those others, with their tiny rods, were pulling in small fry all the time. They couldn't comprehend what Prince Ren was up to, so they ridiculed him. He paid no attention, just focused on waiting for the big one to take his bait.

Finally, one day, the exciting moment arrived: an enormous fish took hold of those fifty cows! The fish bit the enormous hook and quickly disappeared beneath the waves, thrashing in all directions as he dove for deep waters. To try and disengage the bait, he then broke the surface of the water, leaping high and raising his dorsal fin as he whipped his tail. The waves frothed into white peaks as the ocean's waters violently churned about, issuing a terrifying sound that was like the mighty howl of an angry ghost. People thousands of li away heard it and felt its power. Those who had often ridiculed Prince Ren were now cowering in fear, not even daring to look. Prince Ren himself was serene as he gripped his sturdy rod and set the huge fish firmly on the hook. After a mighty battle, the huge fish finally died and Prince Ren pulled it up onto shore.

He had realized his ambition, and caught a huge fish. How big was it, exactly? Prince Ren cut off all the meat and dried it in strips, then gladly passed it out among the people. From Zhe River (today's Zhejiang Province) towards the east, to north of the Nine Yi Mountains (now in Hunan Province), all who were within this vast territory were able to enjoy that fish and eat to their heart's content.

Later, those people who had ridiculed Prince Ren made haste to boast about his prowess as though he was an old friend, exaggerating the story and embellishing it as though they had personally witnessed the whole thing. In point of fact, they continued, as before, to sit by tiny streams with their tiny fishing poles, simply trying to catch tiny fish. When the story reaches this point in the book, *Zhuang-zi* notes sarcastically that people like this will never catch any kind of big fish.

After telling this story, the book goes on to add a comment. Managing affairs of state in a country is similar to the way in which Prince

Ren caught the big fish. It requires far-reaching ideals and powerful strength. Those who have never heard of the methods by which Prince Ren caught his fish unfortunately are vastly under-qualified to run a country.

西施的传说

原文：

máo shī shū zī, gōng pín yán xiào
毛施淑姿，工颦妍笑

故事：

在中国，人们夸赞一个容貌美丽的女性，经常会说“她像西施一样美”。西施是中国古代最有名的美女之一，民间流传着很多有关她的故事。

西施生活在距今两千多年的春秋时代（前770—前476）末期，是当时的越国人。她生长在一个有山有水的村庄，家境普普通通，但她天生丽质，举止优雅，因而十分引人注目。她经常跟女伴们一起到河边去洗衣服，清澈的河水映照出她美丽的身影。据说河里的鱼儿看见她的影子，也被吸引，竟然忘记游动，沉到了河底。从此，人们就用“沉鱼”这个代号来称呼西施。

西施身体柔弱，有心口疼的病。有一次她正走在路上，病又发作了，她用手捂着胸口，艰难地走着，因为痛苦，不由自主地皱起眉头。人们看见她这副模样，都十分同情，纷纷停下来问候她，帮助她回到家里。人们背后议论说，她生病时的这种样子，使她看起来更美。这话被西施邻居的一个女孩听到了，这女孩叫东施，相貌不好看，头脑也比较简单，她听到人们的议论，就想，原来这种样子就是美呀！于是，第二天，这位东施姑娘走在路上的时候，就学着西施的样子，手捂着胸口，皱起眉头，故意慢慢地走。哪知道人们看见她这副样子，不但不过来称赞她，反而都像受了惊吓似的，有人赶紧把门关起来，有人赶紧带着小孩儿跑得远远的。后来，人们就把那种失败的模仿称为“东施效颦（pín，意思是皱眉）”。

可是，西施的美貌并没有给她带来幸福，反而给她带来了不幸。

当时越国在与吴国的战争中失败，越王句（gōu）践也做了吴国的俘虏。后来句践被释放回国，发誓要复仇。他大力发展农业，建立强大的军队，另外，又派大臣到民间去挑选美女，想利用美女削弱吴国的力量。结果，西施就被选中了。她

先被送到越王那里，穿上华丽的衣服，有人教她学习歌舞和各种宫廷礼仪。虽然她不太愿意，但在当时，国王的命令是不能违背的。然后，越王将她送到吴国，献给好色的吴王。吴王马上被西施的美貌迷住了。他不顾手下大臣的反对，坚持留下了西施。

吴王对西施百依百顺，特意建了华丽的宫殿给她住。从此之后，吴王整天与西施在一起玩乐，不理国事。西施按照越王事先的命令，向吴王提出种种奢侈的要求，吴王也都一一答应。时间长了，吴国的国力变得很空虚。这时，越王乘机出兵攻打吴国，将吴国灭亡，吴王也被迫自杀了。

吴国灭亡了，西施也完成了她的使命。然而她并没有回到越国，而是从此消失了。人们猜测，她可能是被生性多疑的越王句践沉入江水中杀害了。

人们很同情西施这个美丽善良的女子，不愿意让她就这样悲惨地离开了人间，于是就编了一个美好的结局，说她与她的恋人，也就是当初将她挑选出来的那位大臣，两人一起坐船逃到了远方，过上了美满的生活。

The Legend of Xi Shi

In China, when people praise the beauty of a woman, they often say that she is as beautiful as Xi Shi. Xi Shi was one of the most famous beauties in Chinese antiquity and many tales about her have been passed down through the ages.

She lived in the latter part of the Spring and Autumn period (770–476 BCE), in what was then the state of Yue. She was born and bred in a small hamlet in a landscape that included both mountains and water. Although her family was not out of the ordinary, she had a natural beauty and an elegant manner that were most appealing. She would often go down to the river to wash clothes with other women, where her loveliness was reflected in the pure waters. It is said that fish would see this reflection and be so entranced that they would forget to move, which made them sink to the bottom. People later used the term 'fish sinker' to describe women of beauty like Xi Shi.

Her constitution was weak, however, and she suffered from painful heart disease. One day as she was walking along the road, a heart attack came upon her and she grasped her chest and moved forward only slowly and with great difficulty, meanwhile knitting her brows unconsciously with the pain. People saw this and instantly moved to help her out of sympathy, and were able to get her back home. There was some controversy after that as to whether she was not even more beautiful in this condition than before. A neighbor of Xi Shi's heard this opinion, someone whose name was Dong Shi (East Shi, whereas Xi Shi's name means West Shi). Dong Shi was not good looking. She was also a

bit simple, and when she heard this she said to herself, "Oh, so that is what beauty is!" The next day, when she went out walking, she intentionally clutched her chest, knit her brows, and moved forward very slowly, trying to mimic Xi Shi. When people saw this shocking sight, not only did they not move to help her but they quickly grabbed children, fled inside, and shut their doors. Later, people began to refer to this kind of foolishness in trying to copy the behavior of someone else as, "Dong Shi knitting her brows."

Xi Shi's beauty did not bring her good fortune, however, but rather misfortune.

At the time, the state of Yue was defeated by the state of Wu in the course of a war, and the king of Yue, Gou Jian, was captured and taken prisoner. He was later released, but he swore to take revenge. In his own country of Yue, he built up agriculture, established a powerful army, and also sent ministers throughout the land to find the most beautiful women. He intended to use these beauties to weaken the strength of Wu. As a result Xi Shi was discovered and first sent to the King of Yue, where she was clothed in beautiful garments and taught the refined arts of music and dance, as well as all kinds of court etiquette. Although she wasn't totally willing to do this, in those days a king's orders could not be refused. The King of Yue then sent Xi Shi to the

state of Wu, where he made a gift of her to the King of Wu. The King of Wu was instantly besotted by her beauty. Ignoring the opposition of his senior advisors, he insisted on keeping her at his side. He did whatever she asked him to do. He built gorgeous palaces for her. He whiled away the time with her and began to disregard affairs of state. As ordered in advance by the King of Yue, Xi Shi made all kinds of expensive demands and was granted every one. Time went on and the strength of the state of Wu evaporated. At this point, the King of Yue mobilized his troops for the attack, he obliterated the state of Wu, and he forced the King of Wu to commit suicide.

With the end of the state of Wu, Xi Shi had accomplished her mission. She did not return to Yue, however. Instead, she simply disappeared. Some suspect that she may have been drowned by the King of Yue, whose character was ever distrustful.

Others are so fond of the kind-hearted and beautiful Xi Shi that they are not willing to allow her this tragic parting from the realm of humans. Instead, they fabricate a different ending and say that she had a lover. He was the senior advisor who had selected her for her beauty at the very beginning. The two of them found a boat and escaped to distant lands, where they led a long and happy life.

Historical Tales

历史故事

姜太公钓鱼

原文：

pán xī yī yǐn ， zuǒ shí ē héng
磻溪伊尹，佐时阿衡

故事：

商朝（前1600—前1046）末年，在周文王的领导下，周国逐渐强大起来。后来，周文王的儿子周武王联合其他部落，讨伐暴虐荒淫的商纣（zhòu）王，将商朝灭亡，建立了周朝（前1046—前256）。姜尚帮助周文王和周武王完成了这一伟大事业，他大器晚成，当他开始辅佐周文王时，已经七十多岁了。

姜尚又叫姜子牙，后来人们尊称他为姜太公。他出生的时候家境贫寒，家里没有办法给他提供良好的教育，更没有可能让他进入朝廷做官。为了谋生，姜太公做过很多工作。他曾经在商的都城里做过屠夫，宰牛卖肉；又曾经在黄河边上的一个渡口卖吃的东西。虽然处境不顺，吃了很多苦，但他始终勤奋学习各种知识，研究治理国家的方法，希望有一天能够获得施展才能的机会，成就一番伟大事业。

当时商王朝政治腐败，社会黑暗，国家日益走向衰亡。姜太公对此很失望。他走了许多地方，发现西边的周国在贤明的君主周文王领导下，人民安居乐业，国家逐渐强盛。他决定

离开商朝，到周国寻找机会。这时他已经年过七十，但仍然不想放弃建功立业的雄心。

姜太公来到周国后，隐居在河边，整天坐在那里摆出钓鱼的样子。但奇怪的是，他连一条鱼也没有钓到。原来，别人钓鱼的钩子都是弯的，上面挂着吸引鱼儿上钩的香饵，沉入水里。而姜太公的钓钩是直的，上面没有挂鱼饵，并不沉入水中，而是离开水面很高。他高高举起钓竿，说："鱼儿呀，愿意的话，你就自己上钩吧！"

有人经过河边，看见姜太公这种奇特的钓鱼方法，就提醒他说，这样的话，永远也钓不到鱼。姜太公笑着说："我不是钓鱼，而是在等着钓王与侯！"那个热心人觉得这个老先生脑子有点问题，回去之后，将这件事当成好笑的事情对周围的人讲。

过了一段时间，这件事传到了周文王那里，引起了他的注意。周文王派人来找姜太公，希望请他去谈一谈。但姜太公不搭理来人，说："大鱼为什么不自己上钩呢？"来人回去报告周文王，周文王决定亲自去见姜太公。他穿得整整齐齐，带着丰厚的礼物来到河边。两人见面之后，周文王请教治理国家的方法，姜太公胸有成竹，将自己思考成熟的一套道理讲了出来。周文王听后非常高兴，认为姜太公正是可以辅佐他治理好周国的圣人。于是，他诚恳地请姜太公马上到他的宫廷里去，姜太公也不推辞，就坐着周文王的车一起走了。

周文王进一步了解了姜太公的才能后，即请他担任周国的最高官职。在周国这个舞台上，姜太公的才能得到了最大发挥，实现了自己的理想。周文王父子对他都很尊敬。周朝建立后，周武王将齐地封给姜太公，后来齐国的君主，就是姜太公的后代。

Jiang Taigong Goes Fishing

Under the leadership of Zhou Wenwang, the State of Zhou became even more prosperous in the waning years of the Shang dynasty (1600–1046 BCE). Later, Zhou Wenwang's son, Zhou Wuwang, was to unify other tribes and mobilize forces to crush the tyrannical rule of the Shang King, Shang Zhouwang. Zhou Wuwang thereby put an end to the Shang dynasty and founded the Zhou dynasty (1046–256 BCE). The man who helped both father and son in this great enterprise was named Jiang Shang. He rose to the challenge at a late age. He was in his seventies when he first began serving Zhou Wenwang.

Jiang Shang is also known as Jiang Ziya, and later generations were to speak of him respectfully as Jiang Taigong, or "Great-grandfather Jiang." He was born to a poor family that was unable to provide any education for him, and even less able to put him forward to the court to serve as an official. He worked at various jobs just to make a living, for example as a butcher in the capital city of Shang, slaughtering cows and selling the meat, and as a peddler of things to eat at a fording spot on the Yellow River. Although things did not always go well and he often ate little, he still was eager to study all kinds of 'knowledge,' to explore the best ways of administering a country. He hoped that one day he might have an opportunity to put his talents to use. He wanted to accomplish something major in his life.

Political life in the Shang dynasty at the time was corrupt, "society" was "dark," and the country was headed for disaster. Jiang Taigong felt that the situation there was hopeless. He had travelled many places and discovered that people in the state of Zhou to the west were living happy lives, working peaceably, under the leadership of a king named Zhou Wenwang. Jiang Taigong decided to leave the Shang state and find an opportunity in the state of Zhou. At this point, he was already over seventy, but he had no intention of giving up his ambition to make a worthy contribution in life.

After reaching the State of Zhou, Jiang Taigong lived alone by the side of a river. Every day he sat on the banks of the river, looking as though he were fishing. The strange thing was that he never caught a fish. People found out that his fish-hook, which normally is curved, was straight, and held no bait. They found out that instead of putting his line in the water, he kept it well above the water, in the air. As he raised his rod, he would say, "Here fish! If you like, please come put yourself on my hook!"

People passing by would see this strange way of fishing and would advise Jiang Taigong that he would never catch a fish in this manner.

He would laugh and say, "I am not going for fish! I am wanting to catch a king and a Duke!" Well-intentioned people decided he must be a little daft. After going home, they start talking about him to all those around as if he were something to laugh about.

After a while, news of this behavior made its way to Zhou Wenwang. Struck by it, he sent people down to find Jiang Taigong to invite him to come talk to the King. Jiang Taigong paid no attention to these minions. "Doesn't the big fish himself want to put himself on the hook?" This was reported back to Zhou Wenwang, who decided that indeed he personally would pay a visit to this man. The King dressed impeccably in his finest clothes and, bearing valuable gifts, made his way to the riverside. After the two people met, Zhou Wenwang asked Jiang Taigong for his advice on administering the country. Jiang Taigong had the ideas fully prepared in his mind. He came forth with principles and actions that had been thought and

were ripe for action. Zhou Wenwang was extremely happy to hear all this, and he knew that Jiang Taigong was a true sage who could help support and run the state of Zhou. He earnestly invited Jiang Taigong to come serve in the court immediately, and Jiang Taigong did not turn him down. The two men promptly sat in the King's coach and left the riverside together.

After Zhou Wenwang became more familiar with the extent of Jiang Taigong's talents, he invited him to serve as the highest official in the state of Zhou. On this stage, Jiang Taigong's talents could be used to the utmost and he could at last realize his ideals. Both father and son, Wenwang and Wuwang, respected him. When the Zhou dynasty was founded, Zhou Wuwang conferred the State of Qi on Jiang Taigong. Later, the sovereign rulers of Qi were all descendants of Jiang Taigong.

伊尹辅佐商汤

原文：

pán xī yī yǐn， zuǒ shí ē héng
磻溪伊尹，佐时阿衡

故事：

夏朝（前2070—前1600）末年，统治者夏桀（jié）过着奢侈放纵的生活，人民遭受残酷的奴役，负担很重，处境悲惨。因为夏桀自比为太阳，他们就诅咒说："这个可怕的太阳为什么还不毁灭呢？我们宁愿与你同归于尽。"

这个时候，有一个部落强大起来，他们的首领叫商汤。商汤对待人民宽厚仁慈。有一次，他看见有人在四个方向都挂起猎捕动物用的网，祈祷说："天上、地下、四面八方来的鸟兽，都掉进我的网里吧。"汤叹息说："这样的话，鸟兽不就灭绝了吗？"他命令那人撤掉三个方向的网，只留下一面，祷告说："愿意往左的，就往左；愿意往右的，就往右；不听我话的，才掉进我的网里来。"

这件事传开后，其他部落的人都说，商汤对动物都这样仁慈，何况对人民呢？于是，投奔商汤的人越来越多，这其中，有一个叫伊尹（yǐn）的贤士。

伊尹是另一个部落的人，很想投奔商汤，可是因为地位不高，他无法直接见到商汤。正好部落首领的女儿要嫁给商汤，伊尹就主动提出，充当她的随从人员。这样，他就来到了商汤的部落。

伊尹负责给商汤和他的新婚妻子准备饭菜，他很快掌握了他们的口味，准备的饭菜引起了商汤的注意。商汤想认识一下这位厨房的负责人，伊尹就带着做饭的工具来到商汤面前。他先从做饭菜的道理讲起，然后将当时的政治、社会状况比喻成做饭菜的情形，讲述他对国家大事的看法，并向商汤提出一些重要的意见和建议。商汤向伊尹请教了更多关于治理国家、对待人民的问题之后，知道他是个了不起的人才，就让他担任最高执政大臣的职位，帮助自己管理国家大事。

在伊尹的谋划下，商汤积极准备灭亡夏朝。伊尹去劝说那些附属于夏朝的部落，向他们指出夏桀的残暴不仁，希望他们接受商汤的命令。有的部落拒绝站到商汤一边，商汤就出兵将他们消灭。于是，商汤的势力进一步壮大。

伊尹向商汤建议，停止向夏朝进贡，以试探夏桀那边的反应。夏桀很生气，马上命令好几个部族的军队征讨商。看到夏桀还有这样的实力，伊尹让汤赶紧向夏桀请罪，并立刻献上了给夏桀的贡品。夏桀觉得人们都害怕自己，变得更加残暴和放纵。

一年之后，那些本来听从夏桀命令的部族也无法忍受他的统治，纷纷背叛。商汤和伊尹知道时机已经成熟，便召集军队，下令讨伐夏桀。商汤向士兵们发表演说，称："并不是我要叛乱，而是因为夏桀有很多罪恶，连上天都想灭亡他了。"他详细列举夏桀的罪行，激发了大家的愤怒，于是商军勇敢地进攻，经过一场激战，取得了胜利，攻进了夏的都城。商汤捉住夏桀，将他流放到南方。夏朝灭亡了，商汤建立了中国历史上第二个王朝商朝。

商汤减轻人民的负担，鼓励他们发展生产，商的统治区域进一步扩展。伊尹一直是商汤的得力助手，在商汤死后，他又辅佐继任的几位国君，成为中国历史上第一个有名的贤相，受到后人尊敬。

Yi Yin Helps Support Shang Tang

Towards the end of the Xia dynasty (2070–1600 BCE), the ruler Xia Jie led a dissolute life, while his subjects suffered from ever more cruel bondage and onerous burdens, to the extent that their situation became dreadful. Since Xia Jie compared himself to the sun, people began to curse him, saying, "Why has this terrible sun not yet been destroyed? We are willing to die too if we can take him out."

One of the many tribes grew more powerful at this time and was headed by a leader called Shang Tang. Shang Tang was generous and beneficent in the way he treated people. One time, he saw people spread a large hunting net in four directions, as they prayed for a good catch. "Heaven above, earth below, all the birds and creatures of the eight directions and four sides, come fall into my hunting net!" Shang Tang ordered the people to cut three of the four sides out of the net. He prayed, "Those who want to go left can go left, those who want to go right, can go right. Those who don't listen to my commands can go ahead and fall into my net."

After this event became known, people of other tribes began to say that if Shang Tang were so good to animals, what must he be in his re-

lations with people? Increasing numbers of people began to surrender to the rule of Shang Tang, and among them was a man of great virtue named Yi Yin.

Yi Yin belonged to a different tribe. He very much wanted to join Shang Tang, but since he was of lowly position there was no way he could come into contact with him. Fortunately, just at that time the daughter of the head of his tribe was being sent in marriage to Shang Tang. Yi Yin voluntarily put himself forward as a bodyguard on the trip. In this way, he arrived at Shang Tang's tribe.

Yi Yin was responsible for preparing meals for Shang Tang and his new bride. He quickly mastered their individual tastes and his creations caught Shang Tang's attention. Shang Tang made it known that he wanted to meet this chef, so Yi Yin came in, together with the tools of his trade. First, he described the principles behind his cooking. From those, he quickly moved to contemporary politics and social conditions. Using the analogies of cooking, he described his views on affairs of state. He raised many important opinions and recommendations to Shang Tang. After Shang Tang asked Yi Yin to educate him on such matters as administering a country, and how to handle or treat the people in the country, he knew that this was a rare talent. He invited him to accept the highest administrative position in the land and become Minister—he asked Yi Yin to help him manage affairs of state.

With the strategic advice of Yi Yin, Shang Tang actively began to prepare for the destruction of the Xia dynasty. Meanwhile, Yi Yin went to the various tribes that were subjects of the Xia and encouraged them to switch allegiance and take orders from Shang Tang. He pointed out the cruel and inhumane behavior of Xia Jie. Some tribes refused to come over to Shang Tang; Shang Tang then mobilized troops and obliterated them. Shang Tang's power grew even greater.

Yi Yin recommended to Shang Tang that he stop sending tribute to the Xia dynasty, in order to test the response of Xia Jie. Xia Jie was furious and promptly ordered a number of tribes into action against Shang Tang. Seeing the real strength of Xia Jie, Yi Yin quickly made apologies to Xia Jie and delivered the tribute. Xia Jie then felt that people were truly afraid of him, which only made him even more tyrannical.

One year later, tribes who earlier had not been willing to come over to Shang Tang were now finding they could no longer endure the rule of Xia Jie. They began to defect in droves. Shang Tang and Yi Yin knew that the moment was ripe to attack; they assembled armies and ordered war against Xia Jie. Shang Tang delivered a speech to the soldiers, in which he said, "It is not that I want to rebel. It is that Xia Jie has committed so many heinous crimes that even heaven above is wanting to get rid of him." He then listed in detail all the crimes of Xia Jie and successfully aroused the anger of the populace. The Shang army then bravely attacked and, after an intense war achieved victory. The Shang armies marched into the Xia capital after which Shang Tang captured Xia Jie and exiled him to the south. The Xia dynasty was destroyed and Shang Tang set up the second dynasty in Chinese history, the Shang dynasty.

Shang Tang helped the people by decreasing the burdens they had to bear. He encouraged them to develop production and he expanded the Shang economy. Yi Yin remained as his capable assistant. When Shang Tang died, Yi Yin then helped support the several monarchs who succeeded in his footsteps, becoming the first famous 'virtuous minister' in Chinese history.

齐桓公称霸

原文：

huán gōng kuāng hé，jì ruò fú qīng
桓公匡合，济弱扶倾

故事：

春秋时期（前770—前476）持续近三百年，这段时间中国大地上诸侯国混战，动荡不安。周王不再拥有权威，只能依附于强大的诸侯国。诸侯国起初有一百多个，经过多年兼并战争，出现了一些大国。这些大国争夺霸权，先后出现了几个称霸的诸侯，第一个就是齐桓公。

齐桓公是周朝开国功臣姜太公的后代，在争夺王位的时候，差点被他兄弟的老师管仲杀死。齐桓公即位后，他的老师劝他说，管仲是无论哪个国家都想得到的杰出人才，如果想称霸天下，一定要重用管仲。于是，齐桓公就让管仲执掌大权，对齐国进行改革，选拔优秀的人才为国家服务，加强军事力量，发展生产，国家逐渐强大起来。因为齐国重用有才能的人，所以很多其他国家的人才也都跑到齐国，增强了齐国的实力。

齐国强大之后，齐桓公就想着称霸的事情。他采纳管仲的建议，打着尊重周天子的旗号，与邻国改善关系，又帮助一些国家赶走威胁他们的游牧民族。齐国在诸侯国中树立了威信，不少国家都愿意与齐国结盟，听齐国的命令。另外，齐桓公还消灭了一些小国。

当时，南方的强国楚国是齐国的主要竞争对手，齐桓公决定讨伐楚国。跟齐国结盟的另外七个国家也派出军队，跟齐军一齐浩浩荡荡杀奔楚国。楚王派使者去见齐桓公，管仲代表齐桓公回答说："楚国不向周王进贡过滤酒用的香草，使周王都没办法进行祭祀，我们来征收这种香草；另外，从前有位周王南巡，在楚国境内坐船出了事，再没有返回，我们要调查这件事。"楚国使者觉得这两个理由都是借口，就回答说："贡品没有及时交纳，是我们国君的过错，我们怎么敢不供给呢？至于那位周王南巡没有返回，这事年代太久了，您还是到水边去问一问吧！"

齐军继续前进，楚王又派大臣屈完到齐军中去谈判。齐桓公命令齐军和那七个结盟国的军队排列成阵势，让屈完跟他坐同一辆车检阅。齐桓公得意地说："如果我率领这些军队作战，谁能够抵挡？如果我让军队攻打城池，哪一座城池攻不下？"屈完回答说："如果您用仁德来对待诸侯，谁会不服从

您呢？如果您动用武力的话，那么我们楚国就把大山当作城墙，把大河当作护城河，您这些军队恐怕也没有用处！”这番话表明楚国的态度，愿意与齐国结盟，但也不惧怕交战。齐桓公要求楚国也与齐国等国建立友好关系，屈完就代表楚国与他们订立了盟约。

虽然没能征服楚国，但从此各国都不敢再得罪齐国。后来齐桓公召集多个诸侯国开结盟大会，周王也派人参加，正式承认了齐恒公的霸主地位。

齐桓公因为取得这样的成就而变得骄傲，生活奢侈放纵，娶了很多个妻子，重用一些品德败坏、只知道讨好他的小人，对管仲的劝告也听不进去了。在他晚年，齐国发生了内乱，他也悲惨地死去。

Qi Huangong Gains Hegemony

The Spring and Autumn period went on for almost three hundred years (770–476 BCE), and was a period of tremendous unrest in which various principalities vied for power. Ostensibly in control, the King of Zhou no longer held ultimate power and had to pay allegiance to the stronger states. At the beginning, there were more than one hundred principalities. After years of warfare and con-

solidation, several stronger powers came to the fore. These now contended for power among themselves; first among these princes seeking hegemony was a man named Qi Huangong.

Qi Huangong was a descendant of Jiang Taigong, minister to the founder of the Zhou dynasty. In his efforts to gain the throne, he was almost killed by Guan Zhong, the teacher of his brother. Once he was on the throne, his own teacher urged him to employ Guan Zhong in an important position and make use of his talents. He noted that Guan Zhong was someone every one of the princes would like to win over, in order to benefit from his outstanding mind. If Qi Huangong wanted hegemony over all under heaven, the teacher went on, he would definitely have to make use of Guan Zhong. As a result, Qi Huangong allowed Guan Zhong to wield tremendous power. Guan Zhong carried out reforms in the country, chose superior talent to work with him, strengthened military power, developed production, and increased the overall power of the country. Since talented personnel were put to good use in the state of Qi, many talented people from other states were attracted to come to it as well.

After Qi became a powerful country in this fashion, Qi Huangong again put his mind to the endeavor of seeking hegemony, ruling all under heaven. In this, he adopted the recommendations of Guan Zhong. Under the banner of respecting the nominal rule of the Prince of Zhou, he improved relations with neighboring countries and even helped some states repulse the threat of nomadic tribes. The state of Qi established a certain authority for itself among other states, and many were happy to join with it in an alliance, that is, to obey its orders. In addition to these activities, Qi Huangong also absorbed some of the smaller countries.

The strong state of Chu in the south now became the main military opponent to the state of Qi. Qi Huangong decided to mobilize war against Chu. Together with his allied armies from seven states, he headed into battle. The King of Chu promptly sent an envoy to meet with Qi Huangong. Representing his sovereign, Guan Zhong responded, "The State of Chu did not pay tribute in the form of a fragrant herb used in the preparation of wine, which has kept the King of Zhou from conducting rituals and ceremonies as required. We are invading in order to obtain this herb. In addition, earlier when a king of Zhou came on a southern inspection tour, by boat, something happened to him while he was within the boundaries of Chu. He never returned. We are investigating that event." The envoy from the State of Chu felt that both of these stated reasons for invading his country were pretexts, so he answered, "That the tribute was not delivered on time was an oversight, for how could we dare not to supply it? As for t that king of Zhou who came on a tour and never returned, that matter happened so long ago that I suggest you make your inquiries beside the river!"

The Qi armies continued their advance, and the King of Chu again sent a minister to conduct negotiations, named Qu Wan. Qi Huangong now ordered the armies of all seven countries in the alliance to array themselves in formation and he had Qu Wan sit together with him in a coach as they went up and down the soldiers' ranks. Quite pleased with himself, Qi Huangong said, "Who could stand up against an army like this? If I lead these troops forth, how could any fortress [fortified city and moat] withstand the charge?" Qu Wan responded, 'If you treat the princes with benevolence and virtue, who will not obey and sup-

port you? But if you use force, then we in the state of Chu will use the mountain ranges to serve as our fortress walls, we will use the rivers to serve as our moat. I'm afraid that even your troops will not be enough to defeat us." This statement expressed the attitude of the state of Chu: it was willing to join in an alliance with Qi but, at the same time, it was not afraid of engaging in war. Qi Huangong now asked Qi to join with Chu and other states in establishing friendly relations, and Qu Wan represented the State of Chu in signing an alliance with them.

Although he had not invaded and conquered the State of Chu, from this time on, no other state dared to offend the state of Qi. Later, Qi Huangong called together all principalities to hold a meeting to cement the alliance. The king of Zhou also sent a representative, which indicated that he formally recognized the position of Qi Huangong as holder of supreme power.

With such success, Qi Huangong now became arrogant and began to live a dissolute life. He took many concubines and surrounded himself with small men as advisors, people of little value who simply toadied to his wishes. He ceased to listen to the advice of Guan Zhong. In his later years, civil war broke out in the state of Qi, and Qi Huangong was to die a tragic death.

商王武丁梦见贤相

原文：

yuè gǎn wǔ dīng
说感武丁

故事：

商汤建立的商朝，后来发生了多次政治危机，都城也搬来搬去，最后搬到殷（在现在的河南省安阳），才固定下来。不久之后，出现了一个志向远大、想让国家取得很大发展的国君，叫武丁。

武丁年轻的时候，父亲派他去民间，与平民一同工作，以了解民间的生活。他当上国君之后，却发现手下没有得力的大臣帮助他实现理想。于是他就把政事委托给大臣管理，自己则到处寻访人才，思考怎样才能改变国家的现状。整整三年的时间，他没有对国家大事发表一句言论，那些出身贵族的大臣们在背后议论纷纷。

三年之后，武丁终于向大臣们开口了。他说，有一天

晚上他做了个梦，梦中见到一位品德和才能都很了不起的贤人。他认为这位贤人是上天送给他的礼物，所以醒来就寻找梦中那个人，但现在的大臣里面，没有一个长得像那个人。他描述那个人的外表，让大臣们替他到处寻找。国君好不容易开口提要求了，那些大臣赶紧动身，到各个地方去找。

不久之后，有人找到了样子像武丁所描述的人，并把他带回武丁面前。令大臣们大为惊讶的是，这个人居然是个在工地上修造土墙的奴隶，名叫傅说（yuè）。武丁见到傅说，说他就是自己梦中所见到的贤人，立即任命他为主管国家大事的大臣。贵族出身的大臣们虽然不愿意让一个奴隶出身的人领导他们，但既然傅说是上天通过梦赐给国君的人才，他们也就不能反对了。

武丁遇到傅说之后，好像完全变了一个人，以前他对国家大事不发一言，而现在他不但开口说话，而且每天都积极地向傅说请教治理国家、使商王朝走向强盛的方法。傅说所说的，每一条都能针对商朝当时面对的难题，所讲的道理也很深刻。武丁为得到这样一位卓越的人才而高兴，说："今后无论早晚，我都要听你的教诲。这就好比我要渡大河，你就是我需要的船；又好比遇到了大旱，你就是我等待的雨水。"傅说意味深长地回答："木材要用墨线比着才能加工整齐，帝王要听从部下的劝谏才能取得成功。"他又对武丁说："将这些道理讲得头头是道并不难，难的是您愿意真正实行它们。"

武丁接受傅说的意见，在各方面都推行了一些具体的改革措施，使商朝达到了一个历史顶峰。在武丁统治中国的几十年时间里，国家开始形成一个完整的行政机构，组成了一支相对固定的庞大军队。他还征服了许多小国，使商朝成为包含众多部族的大国。在武丁时代，商朝的政治、经济、军事、文化都得到空前发展，国力大大增强。我们现在所能看到的商朝时期的青铜器等文物，大都是武丁时代制造的。这个时代的成就，甚至超过商汤统治的时代。而傅说也因为辅佐武丁取得了这些成就，被视为中国历史上著名的贤相。

Shang Wu Ding Dreams of a Virtuous Minister

Shang Tang founded the Shang dynasty, after which a number of political crises erupted and the capital was moved from one place to another, finally settling down in a place called Yin, which is in today's Anyang, in Henan Province. Not long after this, a monarch appeared who had tremendous and far-sighted ambitions for developing the state. His name was Wu Ding.

When Wu Ding was a young man, his father sent him off to live among the people, to work beside them and understand their lives. After he became head of state, Wu Ding discovered that he had no competent ministers who could help him realize his ideals. He therefore handed over governing matters to other ministers while he went around the country, searching for the best people to help him rule. He spent a full three years on the road, and during this time he said not so much as one word about the affairs of the country. Ministers running things, who were all from aristocratic families, did not know what to make of it and all talked behind his back.

Three years later, Wu Ding finally began to talk. He told his ministers that one night he had had a dream. In this dream, he saw a virtuous man of extremely high caliber and talent. He felt that this virtuous man had been sent to him as a gift by heaven, and so when he awoke he went in search of this man. Among the ministers around him, Wu Ding said, he saw nobody who resembled this person. He described the features and build of the person, and asked the ministers to help him in his search. Since it was so rare for the monarch to open his mouth and make a request, the ministers all promptly set out to help. They went searching through all the regions of the state.

Not long after, one Minister found a person who fit the description that Wu Ding had given. The person was brought back and presented to the king. The surprising

thing was that he was actually a slave, who had been found working on the construction of a tamped-earth wall. His name was Fu Yue. The moment Wu Ding saw him, he said that this was indeed the very 'virtuous man' he had seen in his dream. He immediately appointed Fu Yue to manage affairs of state. The aristocratic ministers were not happy to have a slave as their superior, but since Fu Yue had been given to their monarch by Heaven, they could do nothing about it.

Wu Ding was a changed man after meeting Fu Yue. He had said nothing about affairs of state before, but now he was intensely involved, asking Fu Yue daily for advice on managing the country, on how to build the Shang dynasty into a powerful and prosperous state. Everything that Fu Yue said was on target in resolving contemporary problems in the dynasty, and his reasoning was extremely profound. Wu Ding was overjoyed to have been given such an outstanding man of talent. He told him, "From now on, whether immediately or in due course, I will follow your instructions. It is as if I need to cross over a great river, and you are my boat. Or as though I have been in a drought, and you are the rain for which I have been waiting." Fu Yue replied, "Wood needs the guidance of inked lines for it to be cut in a straight and proper way. A ruler needs to listen to the advice of his subordinates to achieve success." He also said to Wu Ding, "These principles are easy to recite. The hard part is to be willing to put them into effect."

Wu Ding accepted Fu Yue's advice and implemented specific and concrete reform measures, which allowed the Shang dynasty to reach one of the heights of Chinese history. In the several decades during which Wu Ding governed China, the country began to form a complete administrative system and to organize a relatively fixed and sizeable army. Wu Ding also subjugated a number of small countries and brought different

tribes under the governance of the Shang, turning it into a multi-ethnic state. During the Wu Ding era, Shang politics, economics, military affairs, and culture reached an unprecedented state of development and the country was greatly strengthened. The Shang bronze artifacts that we see today are mostly the product of the Wu Ding era. The accomplishments of this era even surpassed those of the era of Shang Tang. Having helped Wu Ding achieve these things, Fu Yue is even today regarded as the great "virtuous minister" of Chinese history.

晋献公假途灭虢

原文：

jiǎ tú miè guó
假途灭虢

故事：

晋献公是春秋时期晋国的国君，他即位后吞并一些弱小的诸侯国，使晋国变得比较强大。但晋献公仍然觉得不满足，希望晋国的势力扩张到更远的地方。

在晋国的南面有两个小国，一个叫虞（yú），一个叫虢（guó）。这两个国家地理上是近邻，一直相处得很好。晋献公很想把它们消灭，就借口说虢国得罪了晋国，要去讨伐虢国。可是讨伐虢国，必须经过虞地，怎样才能通过虞国去打虢国呢？晋国大臣荀息向晋献公建议说，虞国国君目光短浅，贪图财物，只要用贵重的礼物贿赂他，就可以达到目的。

晋献公派人带了贵重的玉璧、良马等礼物去见虞国国君，表达要向虞国借路去攻打虢国的意思。虞国国君看到这些礼物，十分高兴，立刻答应了晋国的请求。他不但同意让晋国军队通过自己的国境，甚至还出兵帮助晋国去攻打虢国。结果，晋军攻占了虢国的都城，迫使虢国君臣逃到了黄河南边，将另一个地方当成都城。虞国和虢国的友好关系当然也破裂了。晋军占领了虢国和虞国之间的重要地区，再也不怕这两个国家联合起来对付晋国了。

过了三年，晋献公再次向虞国借路去攻打虢国，这次送上了更加贵重的礼物。虞国的大臣宫之奇阻止国君说："虢国是我们虞国的屏障，虢国灭亡了，虞国也不能长久。上次借路给晋国就已经不对了，怎么能第二次这样做呢？我们和虢国的关系，就如同嘴唇和牙齿一样，是相互依存的；失去了嘴唇，牙齿就会觉得寒冷。"虞国国君辩解说，晋国只是想攻打虢国，不会谋害虞国，宫之奇说："晋国可以灭掉虢国，怎么还会爱惜虞国呢？"虞国国君又辩解说："我献给神的祭品又丰盛又干净，神一定会帮助我。"宫之奇劝他说，鬼神只会帮助那些德行高尚的人；但国君完全听不进去，到底还是答应了晋国借路的要求。

宫之奇见国君如此愚昧，就偷偷带着他的家族离开了虞国，并说："看来我们虞国没有机会再举行年终时候的祭祀了，这一次它就会灭亡，晋国用不着再次发兵。"

晋国大举进攻虢国，虢国终于灭亡，虢国国君逃到周王那儿去了。晋军从虢国回来时驻扎在虞国，虞国毫无防备，晋军乘机发动袭击。结果正如宫之奇所判断的那样，虞国国君被俘，虞国也灭亡了。晋国收回了他们当初送给虞国国君的玉璧和良马，虞国国君失去了一切，落得两手空空。

吞并了虢、虞两国之后，晋国的疆域延伸到了黄河南岸地区，为他们争夺中原霸主的地位奠定了基础。

Jin Xiangong Borrows Passage to Attack Guo

Jin Xiangong was the ruler of the State of Jin during the Spring and Autumn period. After assuming the throne, he absorbed some smaller principalities into his domain, greatly expanding the state's size and power. Unsatisfied with this, however, he wanted to expand Jin rule into more distant places.

The two small countries to the south of Jin were called Yu and Guo. In proximity to one another geographically, these two states were on good terms. Jin Xiangong very much wanted to destroy these states and so he used the pretext that the state of Guo had wronged his state of Jin. To redress this wrong, he intended to go in and wage war on Guo. To advance on the state of Guo, however, he first had to pass across the state of Yu, and how to do this was a problem. A senior Minister named Xun Xi made a recommendation in this regard. He told Jin Xiangong that the ruler of Yu was very short-sighted, he was greedy and corrupt and desired material things, therefore he could be bribed with expensive gifts, and one's objective could be achieved.

Jin Xiangong sent off rare and expensive jade disks, fine horses and other gifts to the ruler of Yu, expressing the desire to borrow pas-

sage through the country in order to attack Guo. The ruler of Yu was quite pleased with these gifts and he immediately agreed to the request. He not only agreed to allow Jin armies to penetrate his country's borders, but even dispatched some soldiers to help Jin attack Guo. As a result, the Jin army attacked and occupied the capital of Guo, forcing the ruler of that state to flee south of the Yellow River and to establish his capital in a different place altogether. Naturally, the friendly relations of the two countries were severed as a result. Jin armies occupied a strategic region between Guo and Yu, and there was no longer any need to worry about these two countries joining in a united front against Jin.

Three years later, Jin Xiangong again requested passage through Yu in order to attack the state of Guo. This time he sent even more valuable gifts. A senior minister in the state of Yu, named Gong Zhiqi, tried to stop his monarch from accepting them, saying, "The State of Guo serves as a protective screen for us, against Jin. If Guo is destroyed, the state of Yu cannot long exist. It was a mistake the last time we allowed Jin passage through our country. How can we make the same mistake again? Our relationship with the state of Guo is as lips are to the teeth, we rely upon one another. If we lose the lips, the teeth will get very cold." The ruler of the state of Yu disputed this by saying that the State of Jin merely wanted to attack Guo, it was not scheming to harm the state of Yu. Gong Zhiqi replied, "If Jin can destroy Guo, why should it feel such warm affection for Yu?" The ruler again disputed this, saying, "The offerings I am making to the gods

are both bountiful and clean. The gods will certainly help me." Gong Zhiqi pleaded with the ruler to change his mind. "The gods will only help those who are virtuous and noble in their dealings." The monarch would hear none of this and, in the end, he again approved Jin's request for safe passage.

Seeing how very foolish his ruler was, Gong Zhiqi secretly departed from the state of Yu, taking his family with him. As he left, he commented, "It looks as though the State of Yu will not be conducting the rites at the end of this year. By that time it will not exist. Jin will not have to send troops out a third time."

The State of Jin mobilized a massive attack on the State of Guo, whereupon the Guo ruler fled to the protection of the King of Zhou. From Guo, the Jin armies returned to occupy the State of Yu. Yu had made absolutely no preparations to defend itself and the Jin armies staged a surprise attack. Just as Gong Zhiqi had foreseen, the ruler of Yu was taken captive and the state was destroyed. Jin retrieved all of the gifts it had bestowed upon the ruler, the jade disks, the fine horses—the ruler of Yu lost all and was left empty handed.

After absorbing the states of Guo and Yu, Jin's frontiers extended to the lands along the southern banks of the Yellow River. This strategic acquisition set the stage for the contest to come, that of assuming the position of supreme ruler over the entire central plains region.

晋文公终成霸业

原文：

jiàn tǔ huì méng
践土会盟

故事：

晋献公晚年的时候，宠信一个妃子，想让她生的小儿子继承王位，他的太子被迫自杀，另外两个儿子重（chóng）耳、夷吾则逃离晋国。

重耳起初逃到他母亲的部族。几年之后，晋献公去世，晋国大臣们杀掉他的小儿子，重耳的弟弟夷吾回国当了王。夷吾担心重耳以后会争夺王位，派人去刺杀他，重耳只好再次逃亡。此后，他到过很多国家避难，有的国家对他很客气，有的国家则拒绝接纳他。他来到楚国，楚王盛情接待他，问他以后如果当了王，打算如何报答楚国。重耳回答说，假如两国发生战争，他将命令晋军撤退九十里，以此报答楚国。楚国大臣子玉觉得重耳很有野心，建议楚王杀死他，但是楚王没有这么做。

重耳最后到了秦国，受到秦王的热情接待。当时夷吾已死，他的儿子做了晋国国君。秦王派军队护送重耳回晋国去，帮助他取代他的侄子，当上了晋国国君，这就是晋文公。晋文公流亡国外长达十九年，登上晋国国君之位的时候，已经六十二岁了。他虽然已是个老人，但仍然想实现称霸天下的愿望。

他即位之后，对以前伤害和背叛过他的人十分宽容，这一来，晋国人士都愿意服从他的命令，替他出力。他采取了很多对国家和人民有利的措施，比如减轻征税，减轻刑罚，救济穷人，发展农业、商业和手工业，奖赏对国家有贡献的人，加强军队，等等。晋国人民安居乐业，国力大大增强。他对其他诸侯国也很讲信用，享有很高的威信。

不久，周国发生叛乱，周王出逃，向晋文公请求帮助。

晋文公派兵平定了叛乱，并护送周王回都城。周王把几个地方赏赐给晋国，以感谢晋文公。这样，晋文公就得到了周王的支持。

晋国希望向南方扩展势力，而位于南方长江中游地区的楚国也想成为霸主，积极向北方黄河流域扩展势力。这两个雄心勃勃的大国之间不可避免地发生了一场争霸大战。

战争开始时，楚军占有优势。楚国的子玉率领楚国大军进攻晋军，晋文公命令晋军向后撤退九十里，表面上是为了兑现当年向楚王的承诺，其实是为了避开楚军的锋芒。晋军撤退到离晋国比较近的地方，会合齐、秦、宋等盟国军队，楚军冒险追击，结果陷入重围，损失了三分之二的兵力，主将子玉被迫自杀。晋军获得了决定性的胜利。

战胜楚国之后，就没有哪一国敢再挑战晋国了。此后，晋文公召集众多诸侯国举行结盟大会，各诸侯国名义上的共同领袖周王也亲自参加聚会，任命晋文公为诸侯之长，并赏赐他黑红两色弓箭，表示他有权自由征伐。这样，晋国就成了诸侯国中的霸主，晋文公终于实现了他的称霸愿望。

晋文公在位九年就去世了，但他给晋国带来了繁荣富强的局面，晋国从此成为春秋时期一个超级大国。

Jin Wengong Finally Seeks Hegemony

In his later years, Jin Xiangong was infatuated with a particular concubine with whom he hoped to father a successor to the throne. His Prince had been forced to commit suicide, and two other sons, Chong Er and Yi Wu, had fled from the State of Jin.

At first, Chong Er fled to his mother's tribe. Several years later, after Jin

Xian Gong had died, senior ministers of the state killed the son that the concubine had born him. Chong Er's brother, Yi Wu, then returned to assume the position of head of state. Yi Wu worried, however, that Chong Er might try to seize power in the future, so he dispatched assassins to stab him to death. Chong Er had no choice but to flee once again. He travelled to many countries to avoid being killed, some of which were very hospitable and some of which refused to receive him. When he came to the state of Chu, the Chu monarch received him with great warmth and asked how Chu would be repaid in the future if Chong Er were eventually monarch. Chong Er replied that if conflict erupted between the two states, he would order the Jin armies to withdraw 90 *li* and thereby repay the state of Chu. A minister of the State of Chu named Zi Yu knew that Chong Er was highly ambitious, and he recommended that the king of Chu simply kill him, but the king of Chu was not willing to do this.

Finally, Chong Er went to the state of Qin, where he was also warmly welcomed. His little brother Yi Wu had died by this time and Yi Wu's son was now ruler of Jin. The King of Qin sent an army escort with Chong Er to protect him as he returned home and helped him supplant his nephew on the throne and become the ruler of Jin. At this point, his official name changed from Chong Er to the famous "Jin Wengong." Jin Wengong had been roaming abroad for nineteen years, and was already sixty-two years old when he took over the throne. Although an old man, he still had the desire to realize hegemony over "all under heaven."

After assuming the throne, Jin Wengong was lenient to those who had harmed him and turned against him. Because of this, the people of the country were willing to obey his orders and to exert themselves on his behalf. He adopted many measures that benefitted the country and the people, for example, reducing taxes, lessening punishment for crimes, developing agriculture, trade, and handicrafts industries, rewarding people who made contributions to the country, strengthening the army, and so on. The people of Jin lived peacefully and happily for a period of time and the power of Jin was greatly increased. Jin Wengong was careful to be trustworthy towards rulers of other principalities, and he enjoyed a high degree of prestige among them.

Not long after this, revolts erupted in the state of Zhou. The ruler fled, and asked Jin Wengong for his help. Jin Wengong dispatched troops to quell the disorder, and protected the Zhou ruler as he returned to his capital. The King of Zhou therefore conferred a certain portion of land to the state of Jin in token of his appreciation. In this fashion, Jin Wengong received the support of the King of Zhou.

Jin now wanted to expand its influence towards the south. The state of Chu, situated in the middle reaches of the Yang-tse River in

the south, wanted to expand towards the north. It also wanted to establish hegemony over the entire region, and it was actively pressing towards the regions of the Yellow River. War between these two mighty and fiercely ambitious states, both aiming for hegemony, was unavoidable.

When the war first began, the Chu armies held an advantageous position. Zi Yu of Chu led the attack, and Jin Wengong ordered his troops to draw back ninety *li*. This appeared to be in accordance with the agreement but in fact it was to evade the sharp front lines of the invading army. When the Jin army had retreated to a position not far from the state of Jin, it could join with the allied armies of states like Qi, Qin, and Song. Chu recklessly pressed the attack with the result that it fell into the trap of being encircled. Two-thirds of its forces were lost and its commanding general, Zi Yu, committed suicide. The Jin army had won a decisive victory.

With the military victory over Chu, no other country dared to test the might of the state of Jin. Jin Wengong assembled princes from all the principalities in a large gathering to formalize the alliance. The King of the state of Zhou, ostensibly the primary ruler, also attended and joined in declaring Jin Wengong to be head of all principalities. In addition, the princes presented Jin Wengong with a two-colored arrow, black and red, that meant that he had the power unilaterally to declare war. The state of Jin thereby became supreme ruler among the principalities. Jin Wengong had finally realized his ambition of hegemony over all under heaven.

Jin Wengong died after being on the throne for nine years, but in that time he was able to turn Jin into a prosperous and powerful nation. Jin went on to become a superpower in the Spring and Autumn period.

Tales of Virtue
美德故事

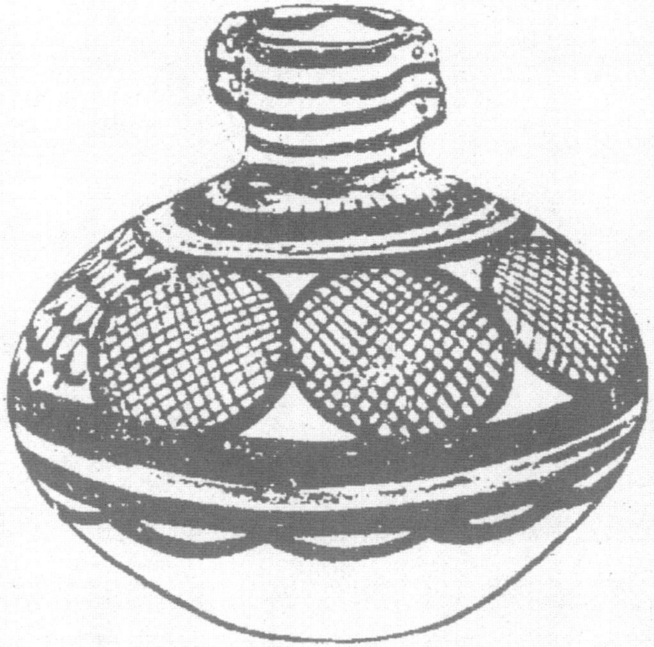

墨子慨叹白丝染色

原文：

mò bēi sī rǎn
墨 悲 丝 染

故事：

墨子是中国战国时期（前475—前221）有名的思想家和科学家，本名是墨翟（dí）。他的学说在当时影响很大，与孔子创立的儒学并称。他痛恨由各国统治者发动的一场又一场的战争，也反对贵族所过的奢侈放纵的生活。他批判当时社会上以强凌弱、互相欺诈等现象，希望人们对待别人要如同对待自己，互相尊重和爱护对方。墨子一生都奔走于各地，推广他的学说，反对兼并战争。

墨子还是一个卓有成就的科学家和高明的工匠，曾经进行各种科学实验，发明和制造了很多机械装置，这跟中国历史上其他的思想家都不一样。

当时最有名的能工巧匠叫公输般，他为楚国制造了一种

叫云梯的攻城装置，楚国打算利用云梯去侵略宋国。墨子听说这件事后，赶了十天十夜的路到楚国去，劝楚王不要攻打宋国。他对楚王讲了一番道理，楚王虽然说不过他，但不愿放弃攻打宋国的计划。墨子于是提出与公输般进行攻城与防御的模拟战争。他解下皮带当作城墙，再拿几块小木板当作武器，与公输般进行了一场精彩的演习，公输般使用了各种方法，都被墨子一一化解了。楚王听说很多墨子的学生正在帮助宋国守城，只好放弃了战争的计划。

墨子平时经常到各种手工作坊去观察和学习。有一天，他来到一家染坊，观看染丝的工艺。工人们把一束束洁白的生丝放进装着各种染料的染缸里，再拿出来时，这些丝就被染成了黄色、黑色、红色等各种颜色，无论怎样漂洗，也无法恢复原来洁白的本色了。墨子看到这种情形，很是感慨，叹着气

说："丝本来都是洁白的，而现在呢，染上黑色的染料就变成青色，染上黄色的染料就变成黄色。染料不同，丝的颜色也跟着变化。染成某种颜色之后，就不能再改成另一种颜色了，可见'染色'这种事必须谨慎小心地进行。"

旁边的人觉得这种事情很正常，没什么好奇怪的。墨子就对他们说，他之所以难过，是由这种现象想到了人性；人的本性也都像生丝一样洁白，进入不同的环境之后，受到各不相同的影响，一旦受到坏的影响，就好比生丝被染错了颜色，再想恢复质朴纯洁的本质，已经不可能了。

墨子后来专门写了一篇文章，以染丝作比喻，说明帝王、诸侯、大臣、知识分子等各种人物必须谨慎地选择自己身边的人员和朋友。那些作出正确选择的人，比如舜帝、大禹、商汤、周武王等人，成为贤明的君主；齐桓公、晋文公、越王句（gōu）践等人则称霸诸侯。而那些作出错误选择的人，比如夏桀（jié）、商纣（zhòu）王等人，则被人民反对，最终国破家亡，被认为是残暴可耻的人。选择不同的"染料"，关系着个人事业的成败、国家的兴亡，所以每个人都应该小心地去选择好的"染料"。

Mo-zi Comments on the Dyeing of Silk

Mo-zi was a famous thinker and scientist during the Warring States period (475–221 BCE). His original name was Mo Dì. His theories and teachings were highly influential at the time, regarded as being on the same level as the Ru School of philosophy founded by Confucius. He deplored the constant state of warfare among principalities and opposed the extravagant and wasteful lifestyles of the aristocracy. He criticized the aggression of the strong against the weak and the mutual deceptions and intrigues that were widely practiced at the time. He wanted people to treat others as they would treat themselves, with mutual respect and an attitude of protecting and caring for the other. Mo-zi spent his life travelling throughout the land, promoting his theories and opposing warfare undertaken in order to expand territory.

In addition, however, Mo-zi was also an accomplished engineer and a scientist with considerable achievements to his name. He carried out many scientific experiments and he also invented and produced a number of mechanical devices, which was quite unlike most other philosophers in Chinese history.

The most famous engineer at the time of Mo-zi was a man named

Gongshu Ban, who had created a device for attacking city walls that was called a Cloud Ladder. The state of Chu wanted to use this Cloud Ladder to invade the state of Song. Mo-zi heard about this and sped over to the state of Chu, spending ten days and ten nights on the road, where he urged its ruler not to attack Song. He explained why. Although the ruler of Chu had no response to his arguments, he still was not willing to give up his plan of attack. Mo-zi then suggested that he and Gongshu Ban simulate warfare right then and there, as though they were the attacker and the defender trying to gain control of a city. Mo-zi took off his belt and used it to symbolize the city walls. He used wooden sticks to represent weapons and he proceeded to perform a dazzling attack on Gongshu Ban. Gongshu Ban in turn used all kinds of defense tactics, every one of which was countered successfully by Mo-zi. The King of Chu learned that many of Mo-zi's students were now in the employ of the Song and helping to guard its city. Seeing Mo-zi's prowess, he realized he had better give up his plan.

Mo-zi often visited the workshops of various small industries in order to observe and to learn. One day, he came to a dye factory and watched the techniques by which the people were dyeing silk. The workers would put pure white skeins of silk into a vat of dyestuff and it would emerge dyed into various colors, yellow, black, red and others. No matter how you washed or treated the silk after that, it would not return to its original lustrous white. Mo-zi observed this, and was moved to comment, "So white at the beginning, look at it now. If you use black dye, it turns green, if you use yellow dye, it turns yellow. Depending on the dye, the color of the silk responds. And after it has been immersed in the dye, it can no longer go back to what it was. It is clear that this process of 'dyeing' must be done with extreme caution."

People standing nearby felt that this was all quite obvious and did not need stating, and that there was nothing very amazing about it. Mo-zi turned to them and said that the reason he felt so strongly about this was that it led him to think about human nature. People's basic nature was like pure white silk but, put in different environments, it changed. Immersed in negative influences, it took on the 'dye,' and never again could return to its original nature.

Mo-zi later wrote a composition that addressed this analogy of dyeing silk. He noted that kings, princes, ministers, intellectuals and indeed everyone should be very careful in choosing people with whom they associate, whether these be in the line of work, or friends. Those who made correct choices, such as Shun Di, the Great Yu, Shang Tang, Zhou Wuwang and others, became virtuous and enlightened rulers. Such people as Qi Huangong, Jin Wengong, and Gou Jian, the king of Yue, were able to extend their rule to other principalities. Those who chose badly, such as Xia Jie, Shang Zhouwang and so on, were opposed by the people and in the end lost their countries and their families. They were regarded as cruel and despicable. The choice of "dyestuffs" is closely related to the success or failure of one's enterprise, the rise or fall of one's country. Each person, therefore, should choose with care.

召公甘棠遗爱

原文：

cún yǐ gān táng, qù ér yì yǒng
存以甘棠，去而益咏

故事：

周武王去世之后，他的儿子周成王即位。这时周成王还是个十来岁的孩子，所以由他的两个叔叔周公、召（shào）公暂时代理朝政。周公和召公都曾经是周武王的重要助手，现在又一起辛勤地工作，把国家治理得井井有条。

当时，周王朝正在营建一座新的都城，称为东都（在今天的河南省洛阳市），召公先去选择好建造宫殿等建筑的地址，并制定建筑规划。他写了一篇很长的劝诫性的文章，总结夏朝、商朝灭亡的历史教训，劝诫年幼的周成王要恭敬谨慎，希望他成为一位贤明的君主。召公说："王刚开始治理国家，拥有一座新建的国都。我唯一的希望是王能尽快推行德政，成为臣民德行的表率，这样天下的臣民才会效法；君臣上下勤勉操劳，我们的国家才会比夏朝、商朝更为长久。"

东都建成之后，周成王让两位叔叔分别治理国家，周公负责管理国家的东部，召公负责管理西部。

召公来到西方，每天勤奋地工作，经常跑到乡村里，察看人们生产、生活的实际状况。地方官和民众有什么事需要他裁决，随时可以找到他。地方官想让他到当地人的房屋里处理公务或休息，他不同意，说："我辛苦一点没有关系，如果让人民辛苦，那就不是仁政。"召公为不打扰民众，经常在野外露宿，在田野或村边的空地上处理事务；感到劳累，他就坐在路边的棠梨树下休息。有时候，他就在棠梨树下审理案件，认真听取原告、被告和证人的话，作出合情合理的裁决。不管是贵族、官员还是平民，他的原则是有罪的人应受到惩处，心怀不满的人应该得到申诉的机会。不少村民就围在他身边，看他怎样处理案件。由于召公体恤民情，推行有利于人民的政策，人民对他非常尊重和爱戴。

在召公和周公的辅佐下，周成王时期成为周代最兴盛的时期。召公去世以后，人们仍然很怀念他，保存好他遗留下的一切东西。随着乡村的发展，要修大路和建新的房屋，召公曾经在下面休息、办公的那棵棠梨树正好在路边，有人主张把它砍掉；但大部人都反对砍树，他们认为应该保留这棵棠梨树，而且要建一座庙，以寄托他们对召公深深的怀念和尊敬。

有人还创作了一首诗歌《甘棠》歌颂召公："枝叶茂盛的甘棠树啊，不要剪削、不要砍伐，召公曾在这下面居住。枝叶茂盛的甘棠树啊，不要剪削、不要毁坏，召公曾在这下面休息。枝叶茂盛的甘棠树啊，不要剪削、不要攀折，召公曾在这下面停留。"这首诗现在仍然保存在中国最早的一部诗歌总集《诗经》里面。

The Birchleaf Pear Tree to Commemorate Shao Gong

When Zhou Wuwang died, his son Zhou Chengwang assumed the throne. Since he was only a child at the time, in his teens, his two uncles temporarily handled affairs on his behalf. They were known as Zhou Gong and Shao Gong. Both had been important aides to Zhou Wuwang and now they again diligently went to work on behalf of his son, managing the country in a conscientious way.

At the time, the Zhou dynasty was just in the midst of building a new capital city. This was called Eastern Capital, or Dong Du, which is today's Luoyang in Henan Province. Shao Gong first went to ascertain the correct places for building palace halls and other buildings, and to confirm the construction plans for the buildings. At the same time, he wrote a long composition of an advisory nature, summarizing the historical lessons of the decline and fall of the Xia and Shang dynasties. He exhorted the young Zhou Chengwang to be respectful and diligent in his work and hoped that he would become a virtuous ruler. Shao Gong said, "Your lordship has just begun to rule the country and you possess a newly build capital. My only hope is that my lord will carry out righteous government as soon as possible, and become the model for virtuous behavior by ministers and people. Only then can all those under heaven, ministers and people, follow the model. Kings and ministers must be conscientious and hard working. Only then can our country last longer than the Xia and the Zhou.

After Dong Du was built, Zhou Chengwang had two able uncles administer the country, Zhou Gong responsible for the eastern part, and Shao Gong responsible for the western part.

When Shao Gong arrived in the west, he worked diligently every day and often travelled to towns and villages to see how people were getting along and ascertain the actual conditions of the people. If local officials and also the people had any issues that needed his judgment, they could find him at any time. Local officials would rather have had him come into their quarters to administer public affairs or else to rest, but he was not willing to do this. He said, "It is fine if I have to work a little harder, but if the people have to work harder, that is not benevolent government." In order not to trouble the people, he often slept outdoors, in a field or on open land near a village. Here he would continue to conduct affairs. If he felt tired, he would sit under a birchleaf pear tree by the side of the road to rest. Sometimes, he would hold court under the birchleaf pear. He would carefully listen to the accused and the prosecution and the words of witnesses, then he would make a judgment that was both rational and emotionally sound. Whether aristocrats, officials, or common people, his principle was that people who had committed crimes should be punished, while those who were dissatisfied with justice should have a chance to bring suit. Many farmers surrounded him as he held court, seeing how he would decide on any given issue. Since Shao Gong deeply understood the feelings of the people, he put forth policies that were beneficial to the populace and the populace in turn regarded him with great respect and love.

Under the help and support of Shao Gong and Zhou Gong, the period in which Zhou Chengwang ruled was the most flourishing in Zhou history. Along with the development of towns and villages, people planned to build a major road and housing along the way to where Shao Gong had once stopped to rest. The birchleaf pear tree turned out to be in the way, and some people advocated cutting it down. Others were opposed to cutting down the tree. They felt it should be preserved

and indeed a temple should be built nearby, to show profound respect and admiration for Shao Gong.

Someone wrote a poem about Shao Gong as well, which said, "Ah, the luxuriant leaves and branches of the birchleaf pear tree, do not prune it, do not cut it, it was under this tree that Shao Gong once resided. Ah, the luxuriant leaves and branches of the birchleaf pear tree, do not prune it, do not destroy it, it was under this tree that Shao Gong once rested." This poem is still preserved in China's earliest compendium of songs and poetry, a book known as *the Shi Jing*, or *the Book of Songs*.

史鱼秉直

原文：

shǐ yù bǐng zhí
史鱼秉直

故事：

春秋时候，卫国有一个大臣叫史鱼，为人正直，被认为是卫国的君子和能够起到重要作用的大臣。当时卫国比较弱小，周围有好几个强国，他一心为国家的事而操劳。

卫国这时的国君叫卫灵公，宠爱一个叫弥子瑕的人。弥子瑕仗着卫灵公的宠爱，常常不遵守法纪，为所欲为。这时卫国还有位贤人叫蘧（qú）伯玉，品德高尚，而且很有才干，卫灵公却不重用他。史鱼看到这种情形，非常担心，多次苦苦劝谏，希望卫灵公多接近蘧伯玉而远离弥子瑕，但卫灵公根本听不进去。

史鱼整天为国事操劳，不幸得了重病。临死的时候，他把儿子叫到身边，悲伤地说：“我是卫国的大臣，却没有能够

将有德有才的蘧伯玉推荐到朝廷，也没有能赶走弥子瑕这种人，身为臣子，没有能够帮助君王走上正确的道路。既然我没有能履行好自己的职责，那么死了之后也不应该享受高规格的丧礼。我死后，你们不要给我举行隆重的丧礼，把我的尸体放在窗户下面就行了。”当时，像史鱼这样的大臣去世后，他的棺木应该放置在房屋中间，接受人们的吊唁。但既然史鱼临终时这样嘱咐，他的儿子也只好按照遗言，将尸体放在了窗户下面。

卫灵公也来吊唁史鱼，看见这种情形，感到很奇怪，就问史鱼的儿子是怎么一回事。史鱼的儿子就将父亲的遗言又讲了一遍。卫灵公听了，很受震动，脸色都变了，悔恨地说：

“这都是我的过错呀！”他下令将史鱼的尸体按礼仪安放。卫灵公知道这是史鱼最后一次劝谏自己，终于接受了史鱼的建议，重用蘧伯玉，并疏远弥子瑕。

孔子听说这件事后，赞叹说："从古到今，有很多敢于直言劝谏君王的人，但人死了，劝谏也就停止了。还没有一个像史鱼这样的，死了以后，还用自己的尸体来劝谏君王，以一片至诚的忠心使君王受到感化。他不就是正直的人吗？"

值得一提的是，孔子与卫灵公、史鱼、蘧伯玉都是同时代的人。孔子周游列国十多年，其中大约十年都待在卫国，而他在卫国的时候，大部分时间都住在蘧伯玉的家中。蘧伯玉是孔子最为尊敬的朋友之一，孔子对他非常了解，对史鱼也很熟悉。《论语》里记载着孔子夸赞史鱼和蘧伯玉的话："史鱼多么正直啊！国家政治清明的时候，他的言行象箭杆一样直；国家政治黑暗的时候，他的言行也象箭杆一样直。蘧伯玉真是一个君子啊！国家政治清明的时候，他就出来做事；国家政治黑暗的时候，他就把自己的才能暂时收敛而隐居起来。"

Shi Yu Holds to the Straight and Upright

During the Spring and Autumn period, the state of Wei had a senior minister named Shi Yu who was upright and honest. He was recognized as a virtuous gentleman and as someone who could be of great service to the state. At the time, Wei was relatively weak and was surrounded by more powerful countries, and Shi Yu bent himself to the task of improving its circumstances.

The monarch of the state of Wei at this time was named Wei Linggong, who was overly taken with a particular councilor named Mi Zixia. Knowing this, Mi Zixia often did not observe the proper laws and discipline, and did essentially whatever he wanted to do. At the same time, Wei had a virtuous gentleman whose name was Qu Boyu, of extremely high caliber and also very capable. Instead of making good use of him, however, Wei Linggong disregarded him. Shi Yu was greatly troubled by this and admonished the monarch many times, advising him to stay closer to Qu Boyu and distance himself from Mi Zixia. But Wei Linggong did not even listen.

Shi Yu worked hard on behalf of the state and unfortunately grew ill prematurely and died. Nearing death, he called his son to his side and said sorrowfully, "I am a senior minister of the state of Wei, and yet I have not been able to install the most able and worthy of men, Qu Boyu, in the court. I also have not been able to rid the court of people like Mi Zixia. Although I am a minister, I have not been able to help my monarch travel the correct path. Since I have not fulfilled my obligations, I should not receive full-scale rites when I die. When I die,

please do not hold an impressive funeral, just put my corpse there under the window." At that time, when senior ministers like Shi Yu died, their coffin was placed in the middle of the room and people came to extend condolences. Since this was Shi Yu's last request, however, the son had to do as he wished. He put the corpse under the window.

Wei Linggong also came to extend condolences and saw this strange situation. He asked the son about it and the son repeated his father's last words in every respect. After hearing this, Wei Linggong was greatly moved, his countenance fell and he exclaimed, "This has all been my fault!" He immediately ordered that Shi Yu's corpse be accorded the highest funeral honors. He knew full well that Shi Yu's last words were in fact his last admonishment to the monarch, and that in the end the monarch would take his advice. He began to lean heavily on Qu Boyu for help, and he distanced himself from Mi Zixia.

When Confucius heard about this, he said appreciatively, "From ancient times, there have been many who dared to speak frankly to their monarchs when giving advice. After a person died, though, the advice died with him. Nobody I have heard about was able, as Shi Yu was, to advise their monarch after death, and especially to use their own corpse as a lesson to the monarch. With ultimate loyalty, he was able to get the monarch to change his ways. Was he not a straight and upright man?"

It is worth noting that Confucius, Wei Linggong, Shi Yu, and Qu Boyu all lived in the same era. In his time spent travelling amongst some dozen countries, Confucius spent around ten years in the state of Wei. While there, he lived mostly in the home of Qu Boyu. Qu Boyu was one of his most respected friends; Confucius knew him very well, and also Shi Yu. *The Analects* contain a phrase that praises both men: "What a straight and upright man was Shi Yu! When the affairs of state were bright and clear, his words and actions were as straight as the shaft of an arrow; when affairs of state were dark and opaque, his words and actions were still as straight as the shaft of an arrow. Qu Boyu was a true gentleman, when politics in the state were clear and bright, he came forth to do his work; when politics in the state were dark and opaque, he kept his own talents to himself and lived a solitary hermetic life."

两疏主动退休

原文：

liǎng shū jiàn jī， jiě zǔ shuí bī
两疏见机，解组谁逼

故事：

“两疏”指的是西汉时期(公元前206—公元25)的疏广与他的侄子疏受，他们的家乡在现在的山东省枣庄市。

疏广从小勤奋好学，在家乡教孩子们读书，因为他教学的水平高，连很远的地方也有人来向他求学。后来汉宣帝为太子选拔老师，听说疏广的名声后，就把他选去当太子的老师。他的课讲得很好，

汉宣帝对他非常满意。疏受是疏广哥哥的儿子，谦恭谨慎，才学和口才都很出众，也通过考试来到太子身边任职；汉宣帝与他交谈之后，大为欣赏，就让他跟叔叔疏广一起担任太子的老师。这样，两疏就共同辅助太子。他们除了给太子讲授儒家的典籍之外，还负责教导太子如何做人，如何正确地治理国家。太子每次去拜见皇帝时，两疏都跟随前往，疏广走在前面，疏受走在后面，大家都认为这是很荣耀的事情。

不知不觉，两疏当太子的老师已经五年，太子也长大了。有一天，疏广对疏受说："听说老子讲过这样的话，一个人懂得知足，就不会遭受耻辱；知道走到哪儿应该停下来，就不会有危险。老子还说过，功成身退，是合乎自然规律的。现在我们已当了很大的官，功成名就，再不走，恐怕以后会后悔。不如我们叔侄一起回家养老，安度晚年，好不好？"疏受恭敬地说："我同意您的意见。"于是两个人就以生病需要回家乡休养为理由，请求皇帝批准他们退休。

汉宣帝和太子因为两疏确实年老多病，就批准了他们的请求，并赏赐给他们许多黄金。在中国古代，一般人做了官之后总是贪图富贵，年龄很老了也不愿意退休，像两疏这样主动退休回乡的人很少。在两疏离开京城回乡那天，朝廷官员和他们的朋友纷纷赶来送行，送行的人所坐的车就有几百辆。两疏辞别众人走了以后，路旁看到这种场景的人都说："这两位大臣真是了不起！"有人还感动得叹息流泪。

疏广与疏受回到故乡后，天天在家里设宴款待亲朋好友，乡邻们有了困难，他们也慷慨资助。过了一年多，他们的子孙觉得这样下去钱会花光，就委托疏广尊敬爱戴的一位老人劝说疏广："天天这样吃喝，钱都要花光了，应该留下一些钱为子孙购置产业。"疏广回答说："我难道真的老糊涂了，不为子孙着想吗？我们家原来就有些房屋和田地，只要子孙辛勤工作，足够过普通人的生活了。如果给他们置办多余的田地房屋，只能让他们变得懒惰松懈。如果他们有才德，过多的钱财容易消磨他们的意志；如果他们愚昧无知，过多的钱财容易增加他们的过失。我们何苦留下很多钱，反而害了子孙呢？"家族里的人这才知道他们的用意，转而心悦诚服地接受了疏广、疏受的做法。两疏就这样活到老，正正常常地去世。

The Two Shu's Voluntarily Retire

The two Shu's refer to Shu Guang and his nephew Shu Shou, of the Western Han period (206BCE–25AD), both of whom lived in what is now Zaozhuang City in Shandong.

From an early age, Shu Guang loved studying and was very diligent. Later, he in turn taught children in his hometown. People came from far away to learn from him due to the high standards he maintained as a teacher. When the emperor of the Han dynasty, Han Xuandi, was looking for a teacher for the Prince, he heard about Shu Guang and chose him to come teach at the court. Shu Guang taught well and Han Xuandi was pleased with him. Shu Shou was the son of Shu Guang's elder brother. He was modest, courteous, and prudent in his behavior, and outstanding in both scholarship and common sense. After taking an exam, and having an audience with the emperor, which was favorable, he too was asked to join his uncle in teaching the Prince. In this way, two Shu's worked together. In addition to lecturing on Ru-school classics, they were responsible for guiding the Prince in proper deportment as an upright person, and in how to manage a country in the correct fashion. Every time the Prince went to pay his respects to the emperor, the two Shu's would accompany, both going and coming. Shu Guang would walk in front and Shu Shou in the rear and everyone felt that this was a most glorious thing to see.

Time went on. Before they knew it, the two Shu's had taught the Prince for five years already and he had grown into a man. One day, Shu Guang said to Shu Shou, "It is said that Lao-zi once observed, 'When a man understands 'enough,' he will not be subject to ridicule. When he knows where he should stop, he will not be in danger.' Lao-zi also said, 'when meritorious service is done, it is time to retire—this is in accord with the laws of nature.' By now, we have served as high officials, have done our duties and made our fame. I fear we will regret it if we do not bow out gracefully at this point. Best for us both to retire, go home to tend to our old age. What do you think?" Shu Shou respectfully answered, "I agree with your opinion." The two Shu's then announced that they were ill and had to go home to recuperate, and in this way they received permission from the emperor to retire.

In fact it was true that the two Shu's were elderly and not well, so Han Xuandi and the Prince not only agreed to their request but bestowed upon them a certain amount of gold. In ancient times in China, most people who served as officials became greedy and were unwilling to retire despite old age. For the Shu's to take it upon themselves to retire voluntarily and leave for the countryside was a rare occur-

rence. On the day they left the capital, officials of the court and friends all came to send them off in a long stream of coaches. The line was several hundred coaches long. Bystanders who witnessed the departure of the two Shu's exclaimed in admiration, "There go two great men!" Many even were moved to tears.

After Shu Guang and Shu Shou returned to their homeland, they invited friends and family in to dine with them every day. Whenever anyone in the locality ran into problems, they were happy to provide funds to help. After a little over one year, their sons and grandsons began to feel that they would soon run out of money if they went on in this way. They therefore asked an elderly gentleman who was highly respected by the two men to approach Shu Guang and say, "Eating and drinking every day like this, the money will be gone. You should leave a little for your sons and grandsons to establish themselves in life." Shu Guang replied, "Do you think I am truly so foolish that I have stopped considering the future of my sons and grandsons? Our family only had a few rooms and a few fields to start with. If the sons and grandsons work hard, these should be plenty for a regular life. If I buy more fields and houses for them, it will only make them slacken off and be-

come lazy. If they are truly talented, then too much money will simply dull their ambition. If they are stupid, then too much money will simply enhance their faults. If we work hard to leave them more money, won't it hurt them all the more?" With this, the family understood their way of thinking, and they happily agreed and supported them in this handling of affairs. The two Shu's lived to be an old age and they died normal deaths.

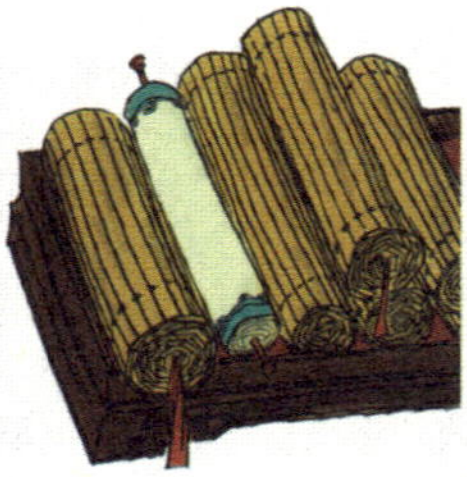

Tales of Talents
人才故事

欧冶子铸剑

原文：

jiàn hào jù què
剑号巨阙

故事：

早在春秋时代的末期，中国人就开始发展冶炼钢铁的技术，并且用钢铁来制造农业工具和剑等武器。当时南方的吴国、越国、楚国出现了一些技艺精湛的制剑工匠，欧冶（yě）子就是其中一位铸剑高手。

欧冶子是越国人，生活在列国纷争的年代。他在制造武器和农具的过程中，发现了钢铁具有与以前使用的青铜等材料不同的性能，可以制成锋利的剑。经过反复试验和深入研究，他终于掌握了铸制铁剑的工艺。

在当时的生产条件下，冶铁制剑属于非常高难的技术，为了造出一把好剑，工匠试着将自己的头发、指甲等投进冶铁的炉中，有时甚至牺牲生命，自己跳进炉火中。即使是欧冶子这样的高手，每次制剑时也必须到处寻找合适的原材料和水，小心谨慎地对待每一个环节，专心致志地工作，通常要花好几年时间才能制作出几把高质量的剑。在一般人眼里，铸剑是很神秘的事情，所以人们将铸剑的过程描述得非常神奇。

越王句（gōu）践拥有五把宝剑，请善于鉴别剑的薛烛来看。薛烛眼光非常高，看了几把世人公认的宝剑，都认为不是真正的宝剑。后来越王让人出示另一把剑，薛烛看到之后，脸

色马上变了，露出又惊喜又惧怕的神情，仔细观察这把剑，问越王是不是欧冶子制造的，越王回答说正是如此。越王说，有人想用好几座城市、上千匹骏马来换取这把宝剑，薛烛认为不能将剑换给对方。他向越王说，欧冶子当初铸造这把剑时，发生了很多神奇的自然现象，天上的神灵都纷纷赶来相助，而欧冶子也施展出了最高的技艺，费尽心力，才造出几把大小不同的宝剑。后来诸侯之间为了争夺这些宝剑，发生了多次战争。现在那些自然现象已不存在，天上的诸多神灵不再降临人间，而欧冶子也快要死了，这样的宝剑再也造不出来，无论多么贵重的财宝，都不足以交换它。

后来楚国强大起来，吞并了越国。楚王早已听说欧冶子的大名，于是派使者带着贵重的礼物去找欧冶子和另一位铸剑高手、吴国的干将，请他们为自己制造宝剑。欧冶子和干将接受了这个请求。他们找到一座山，凿开山石，得到了适合铸剑的溪水；又寻找来上等的铁矿石，将它冶炼成优质的钢铁，打造成三把宝剑。楚王得到这三把宝剑，非常高兴，将它们珍藏起来。

欧冶子所制造的宝剑具有巨大的威力，在水上可以砍断巨大的龙舟，在陆地上可以刺穿坚固的甲胄，是各国国君都想得到的利器。晋国的晋郑王听说楚王拥有三把宝剑，就要求楚王转让给他，楚王当然不答应。晋郑王不顾一切，率军来围攻楚国，战争持续了三年。最后楚王拿出三把剑中的一把，挥舞着它攻击晋军，结果晋军根本无法抵挡，死伤无数；晋郑王感受到这把剑的威力，头发都变白了。晋郑王遭到惨痛的失败，从此不敢再打宝剑的主意。尽管如此，在那个时代，拥有一把欧冶子制造的宝剑，仍然是很多国君和将军的梦想。

Ou Yezi Forges a Sword

As early as the end of the Spring and Autumn period, Chinese began to develop the technology of forging steel, and to use it for making farming tools and such weapons as swords. Artisans with exquisite command of steel-forging technologies were found particularly in such southern states as Wu, Yue, and Chu. Among them, a man named Ou Yezi was a master at forging swords.

Ou Yezi was from the state of Yue and he lived in an era of fragmented political power and conflict. In the process of crafting weapons as well as tools, he discovered that the nature of steel differs from bronze and other metals, and that steel can be used to forge extremely sharp blades on swords. After constant experimentation and extensive research, he finally mastered the art of forging steel.

Given the conditions of the time, forging steel into swords was a difficult and rare art. In order to make a fine blade, artisans tried all kinds of methods including throwing their own hair and finger nails into the molten metal, and sometimes even throwing in themselves. Even such a master as Ou Yezi had to go in search of the best materials when he began to make a sword. He had to take extreme care in handling every link in the process, put his heart into the work, and often spent years before he could produce a truly high-quality sword. To most people, forging a sword was a mysterious process, which is why it was often described in such magical terms.

The King of Yue, Gou Jian, owned five precious swords and he asked a person named Xue Zhu to come appraise them, a man known for his excellence in this field. Xue Zhu had a very discerning eye, and when he saw the swords that others had said were precious, he could see that they were not. The King of Yue then brought forth another sword, at which Xue Zhu's countenance lit up with both delight and fear. He examined it closely and asked the King of Yue if this were not a sword forged by the famous Master, Ou Yezi. The King of Yue confirmed that it was. He went on to say that someone wanted to exchange it with him for several cities and several tens of thousands of fine steeds. Xue Zhu advised him not to make the trade. He said that strange natural phenomena occurred when Ou Yezi first began forging this sword, and spirits from the heavens came down to help. Ou Yezi employed the highest technologies. He did everything in his power and was able to forge several swords that were of different lengths. Later, a number of wars were fought over these swords as contending princes tried to obtain them. Now, the natural phenomena do not exist, heavenly spirits are no longer coming down to earth among humans, and Ou Yezi himself was soon going to be dead. Therefore, said Xue Zhu, swords like this would no longer be made. No matter how great the treasure that was being offered, it was not enough to exchange for this sword.

Later, the state of Chu gained in power and expanded, and was able to absorb the state of Yue into its own territory. The King of Chu had long since heard of the fame of Ou Yezi, and he sent emissaries with expensive presents to Ou Yezi as well as another master of forging swords, Gan Jiang, to ask them to forge some swords for him. Ou Yezi and Gan Jiang agreed to this request. They found a mountain which produced the appropriate spring water, once they had cut through its stone and released the water; they found high-quality iron ore and smelted excellent steel, out of which they forged three precious swords. The King of Chu was overjoyed to get these swords and he carefully stored them away.

The swords forged by Ou Yezi had such force that, on water, they could cut straight through a long boat, and, on land, they could pierce the toughest armor. They were weapons that every country's ruler wanted to obtain. King Jin Zheng of the state of Jin heard that the King of Chu had three precious swords, and he asked him for one of them. Naturally, the King of Chu refused. Disregarding all else, the King of Jin then led his troops in an encircling attack on Chu and the war went on for three years. In the end, the King of Chu took one of the three swords out and, wielding it in his own hands, he counter-attacked. The result was that the Jin army had to fall back, suffering countless deaths and wounded among its troops. It is said that Jin Zheng's hair turned white when he finally realized the mighty force of this sword. Having encountered such a tragic defeat, he did not dare raise the subject of the sword again. Despite this, it remained the dream of many monarchs and generals to be able to own a sword that Ou Yezi had forged.

王充街市读书

原文：

dān dú wán shì　　yù mù náng xiāng
耽读玩市，寓目囊箱

故事：

王充，中国东汉（25—220）时杰出的学者、思想家。他的家乡在现在的浙江省。他们家祖祖辈辈都喜欢用勇力解决问题，经常与别人结下仇怨。可是等到王充出生，家人发现他是个不一样的孩子。

王充小时候跟小伙伴在一起，不像别的孩子那样打闹。小伙伴们都喜欢捉鸟、捕蝉、爬树等，王充却不玩这些。他很懂礼貌，不爱说话，小小年纪就像个成年人。他的父亲觉得很惊奇，于是送他去上学。跟他同时在学校的孩子有一百多个，有人因为犯了错误而遭到责打，有人因为字写得难看而被惩罚，只有王充没有这种经历。后来他又开始学习《论语》和《尚书》这样的儒家经典，每天能背诵一千字。他的学识越来越丰富，品德良好，受到大家称赞。可是王充的性格有点不合群，如果没有遇到志同道合的人，他就整天不说话。他喜欢独立思考，所说的很多言论，别人都觉得奇怪。他仰慕古人蘧（qú）伯玉和史鱼的品行，希望像他们那样做人做事。

在家乡生活到十八岁，王充决定到京城洛阳（在现在的河南省）去继续深造。洛阳是全国政治、经济、文化中心，在那儿有一所太学，是国家最高的学府，里面有很多有名的学者，为国家培养人才。王充来到洛阳后，进入太学学习。他尊重老师，却并不盲目接受他们的思想和见解。除了跟着太学里的老师学习，他还访问居住在洛阳的其他学者，广泛阅读诸子百家的著作，观看朝廷里举行的大型礼式，进一步开阔了眼界，增长了学问。

王充渴望读很多书，恨不得将所有的书都看完，但因为家境不富裕，他无力购买很多书；时间一长，太学里的藏书也显得不够了。怎么办呢？他发现洛阳城里有一些书店，出售各种各样的书籍。他就跑到书店里去看书，店里摆的那些要卖的书，他看一遍就能背诵记住。他看书很专注，仿佛他不是在热闹的街市上，而是在一间安静的书房里。就这样，他逐渐通晓了各家各派的学说。后来，王充又回到家乡，一边教书，一边继续研究各种典籍。他曾经担任过一些小的官职，因为不愿迎合当时的社会风气，最后还是辞职回家了。

王充发现当时流行的书籍和社会上流行的说法里有许多不妥当的地方，于是闭门思考，谢绝一切应酬活动，打算写一部著作澄清这些问题。他写作的时候，窗户、墙壁等地方都放着刀和笔，方便随时写作。经过长期努力，他终于写成了重要的著作《论衡》。

Wang Chong Reads out on The Street

Wang Chong was an outstanding scholar and thinker during the period of Eastern Han (25–220). His home was in what is now Zhejiang Province. For generations, his family had enjoyed resolving problems through use of brute strength, and often made enemies of others as a result. Shortly after Wang Chong was born, his family could see that he was different.

When he was small and playing with friends, Wang Chong was unusually quiet. While others liked to go out and catch birds, cicadas, climb trees and so on, Wang Chong did not. He was extremely courteous and rarely spoke and, even as a child, his behavior was that of an adult. His father felt this was of interest, so he sent him on to school. Among the more than one hundred other children in the same school, many were criticized for making mistakes, some wrote things incorrectly and were punished, while only Wang Chong was free of such problems. Later, when he began to study *the Analects of Confucius*, *the Shang Shu* and other classics of the Ru school of philosophy, he would memorize and be able to recite one thousand words every day. He became very learned, his qualities as a person were excellent and he was highly commended by all. Nonetheless, his character was simply not like others. If he did not meet up with someone with whom he felt in sympathy, then he went all day without saying anything. He liked to think independently, even though others regarded this as very strange. He admired the qualities of such people as Qu Boyu and Shi Yu, and hoped that his conduct as a person and his accomplishments could be like theirs.

Wang Chong lived in the countryside for eighteen years, then decided to come to the capital city of Luoyang (in today's Henan Province) to further his studies. Luoyang was a political, economic and cultural center. A school there called "Tai Xue" was the highest institute of learning in the land. Many famous students studied at this school as its purpose was to nurture talent for the country. After Wang Chong came to Luoyang, he entered Tai Xue for studies. He respected his teachers but did not blindly follow their thinking and views. In addition to studying with teachers at the Tai Xue, he also paid calls on other scholars who were living in Luoyang. He read widely among the works of various schools of thought from the pre-Qin times to early Han, and he observed the rites performed at court, further opening his mind to new things and increasing his knowledge.

Wang Chong had an intense desire to read more books. He wished he could read all books that had been written, but his family was not wealthy and he had no ability to buy books. In due course, he had read everything that the library of the Tai Xue had to offer. He now discovered that Luoyang had some bookstores out on the streets that sold all kinds of books. He would visit these and read a volume right then and there, committing it to heart. He was so focused on reading that he was oblivious to being on a street: he read as though he were in the quiet stillness of a library. In time, he became thoroughly versed in the

theories of all schools of thought. Later, he returned to his homeland and both taught and continued his own research into the classics. He served as an official briefly, but found that he was not willing to accept the social tenor of the times, and in the end he retired and went back home.

Wang Chong discovered that there were many things he disagreed with in popular books at the time and popular ways of thinking in society. As a result, he shut himself into his study and devoted himself to pure thought. He refused all invitations and intended to write a book that explored certain things. He put knives and pen by the window, walls, anyplace convenient so that he could jot things down at any time. After hard work, over a long period of time, he finally finished the major work that is called "*On Measuring Things*."

嵇康弹奏《广陵散》

原文：

jī qín ruǎn xiào
嵇 琴 阮 啸

故事：

三国时代，魏国有七位名士，经常在竹林里面饮酒聚会，他们都崇尚老庄思想，蔑视世俗社会的礼法，被称为“竹林七贤”。嵇（jī）康是“竹林七贤”的领袖，他也是当时有名的文学家、音乐家和哲学家。

当时，魏国掌握实权的是司马昭，他打算从魏国君主曹氏的手中夺取政权。嵇康的妻子是曹氏家族的，他本人对司马氏的做法也很不满。司马昭曾经想请嵇康在他手下做官，嵇康拒绝了。嵇康还经常借题发挥，发表一些愤世嫉俗的言论，以此反抗司马昭等人。

嵇康不喜欢做官，喜欢锤打烧红的铁，打造各种器具。司马昭部下有个高官叫钟会，就是著名书法家钟繇（yóu）的儿子。钟会想结交嵇康，就带着很多随从，穿得整整齐齐去见嵇康。而嵇康穿着工匠的衣服，与一个朋友在树荫下打铁，不理睬钟会他们。钟会等了很久，嵇康连看也不看他一眼，他很愤怒，率领部下转身而去。这个时候，嵇康才开口问他："你听到了什么跑到这儿来，又看到了什么决定离开？"钟会回答："我听到我所听到的，所以跑到这儿来；我看到了我所看到的，所以我决定离开。"钟会回去之后，就对嵇康怀恨在心。

后来发生了一件事，嵇康有个好朋友，被哥哥诬陷犯有不孝顺父母的过错，受到审讯。嵇康知道那个哥哥才是有罪的人，就出面为朋友作证，结果也被囚禁了起来。嵇康曾经得罪过的钟会等人这时候都在背后说嵇康的坏话，劝司马昭借这个机会除掉嵇康。

嵇康在社会上拥有很高声望，他入狱后，很多人都为他鸣不平，还有不少人要求与他一起住在监狱里，认为这是一种荣耀。然而嵇康和他那个朋友最后还是被判处了死刑。

行刑的那天，三千名太学里的学生集体请愿，请求当局赦免嵇康，希望让嵇康来太学做老师，将他的学问和音乐技艺传授给他们。但司马昭为首的权贵拒绝接受这些要求。

嵇康是个身材高大、仪表堂堂、很有风度的美男子。临刑前，他神色自然，如同平常一样。他回头看了看太阳的影子，知道离执行死刑还有一段时间，就要来他的琴，在刑场上当众弹奏了最擅长的《广陵散》。《广陵散》是一首旋律激昂慷慨的音乐，嵇康演奏这首乐曲的水平已达到很高的境界。演奏完毕，他把琴放下，叹息说：“从前有人想跟着我学习弹奏《广陵散》，我没舍得传授。可惜啊，从今以后，演奏《广陵散》的技艺就要失传了！”嵇康从容地接受了死刑，这一年他才四十岁，许多人都为他的死而感到悲痛。

Ji Kang Plays the Qin

During the Three Kingdoms period, the state of Wei had seven gentlemen who frequently got together in a bamboo grove to drink wine. They admired the works of Lao-zi and Zhuang-zi and despised the strictures of the common world. They became known as the "Seven Sages of the Bamboo Grove." Ji Kang was the leader of these seven sages. He was a famous literary figure in his day, as well as a philosopher and a musician.

The person wielding actual power at the time in Wei was Sima Zhao. He intended to wrest the throne from the ruler of Wei, Cao Shi. Ji Kang's wife was of the Cao Shi family and she herself was quite discontent with how Sima Zhao was behaving. He once asked Ji Kang to serve on his staff, and Ji Kang refused. Ji Kang also frequently wrote things about the undesirable ways of the world that were in fact pointed at such people as Sima Zhao.

Rather than being an official, what Ji Kang really liked to do was hammer away at a red-hot piece of metal, crafting it into various things. One of Sima Zhao's subordinates was an official named Zhong Hui who, indeed, was the son of the famous calligrapher Zhong

You. He wanted to make the acquaintance of Ji Kang, so he dressed up properly in full regalia and led a retinue of people to pay a formal call. Ji Kang was dressed in his working clothes and was hammering iron under the shade of a tree with a friend. He did not even glance up when Zhong Hui approached. Zhong Hui waited a long time, getting more and more upset, and finally turned to leave. Only then did Ji Kang deign to speak to him. "What did you hear that you came out here, and what did you see that made you decide to leave?" Zhong Hui replied, "What I heard, is what I heard, and what I saw, is what made

me decide to leave." With that, he turned and left and thereafter held a strong grudge against Ji Kang.

An event was later to occur. Ji Kang had a good friend who was framed, unjustly accused by his brother of being unfilial to his parents, and he was then interrogated. Ji Kang knew that the brother was in fact the wrongful one and he came forth to testify on behalf of his friend. As a result, he too was locked up. At this point, Zhong Hui and others that Ji Kang had offended in the past began to speak against him behind his back, and Sima Zhao too realized that this was an opportunity to get rid of him.

Ji Kang was beloved among the people and many came forth to offer to stay in jail with him, regarding this as a great honor. Nevertheless, in the end Ji Kang as well as the wrongly accused friend, were both sentenced to death.

On the day of execution, three thousand students from the Tai Xue school staged a mass appeal, asking that Ji Kang be pardoned. They asked that he be allowed to come teach at the school, to pass on his great learning and his knowledge of music. As the one in power, Sima Zhao refused this request.

Ji Kang was very tall, with an erect bearing and handsome demeanor, and he was relaxed and calm as the time of execution approached. By seeing the angle of the sun, he knew that there was still some time before the proceedings, and he asked that his qin be brought to him. Before the assembled masses, right there on the execution ground, he began to play the melody known as "Guangling San." The music was rousing and impassioned, and Ji Kang played it with the highest degree of artistic expression. When he had finished, he put the qin aside and said, "People wanted to learn this piece from me in the past and I wasn't willing to let it go. How unfortunate! Now it is lost to the world." Ji Kang went to his death with calm dignity. He was only forty years old, and many there were who wept that day.

马钧巧制水车

原文：

jūn qiǎo rén diào
钧巧任钓

故事：

三国时期，各个领域都人才辈出，其中有一位杰出的发明家和能工巧匠，他就是魏国人马钧。

马钧出身贫寒，不太喜欢说话，但是他喜欢读书，爱思考问题，对机械制造方面的问题特别感兴趣。他经常亲自动手制作各种机械装置，有高超的技能，这为他的发明工作打下了良好的基础。他早年生活贫苦，接触到很多劳动者，对他们繁重的劳动很同情，因此他的发明创造，很多都是对生产工具的改进。

他的第一项重要发明是改革提花织机，当时人们用这种织机织一种表面光洁的提花丝织品。这种机器结构笨重，操作起来很不方便，织工辛辛苦苦工作一个月，才能织出一匹提花丝织品。马钧经过仔细观察、研究，发现这种丝织品的花色、图案有许多是对称重复的，为此，他经过反复试验，简化原来的织机结构，使生产效率大大提高。后来魏明帝赠送给外国使者很多这种丝织品，就是用马钧改进后的织机织成的。

马钧曾在魏国京城担任低级官职。有一天，他和几位高级官员辩论古代到底有没有指南车，高官们认为古书上关于指南车的记载都不可靠，马钧则认为古人有可能曾经制造过这种利用磁铁来指示方向的装置。最后，为了证明自己的观点，他决定亲自制造一部指南车。他刻苦钻研，在工匠们的帮助下，没有多久就制成了指南车，与古书上记载的很相近。这样，关于指南车的争论就以马钧的胜利而结束了。此后，很多人都知道了他的才能和技巧。

马钧最有名的发明是一种用于农业灌溉的提水翻车。当时人们提水的工具主要是桔槔（jié gāo）和辘轳（lù lu），前者利用杠杆原理，后者利用轮转原理。但这两种工具都不能连续运动，提水的效率比较低。马钧住在洛阳的时候，发现一片土地适合种菜，但这片土地地势比较高，怎样才能省时省力地解决浇水灌溉问题呢？他不断试验、探索，终于设计制造出新的灌溉机械——翻车。人站在架子上踏动踏板，就可以带动大轮轴，把水连续不断地从低处送到高处。这种翻车结构精巧，操作方便，连儿童都能转动，受到人民欢迎，很快就到处都推广使用了。后世的人们对这种机械又作了各种改进，在近代水泵发明之前，翻车是最先进的提水工具。直到今天，人们仍然可以在某些地方看见这种水车。

马钧还有许多其他的发明设想，可惜由于当时的统治者不太重视，这些设想大部分未能实现。但人民享受到他的发明创造带来的好处，对他很钦佩，称赞他是天下驰名的巧手。

Ma Jun Crafts a Water Wheel

During the Three Kingdoms period, people of great talent appeared in many fields of endeavor, and among them was an outstanding inventor, and ingenious craftsman by the name of Ma Jun, from the state of Wei.

Ma Jun came from a poor family. He didn't like to talk, but he did like to read books and he liked to think things over. He was particularly intrigued by mechanics and just how things worked. He often made various mechanical devices by hand and developed considerable expertise, which helped lay a foundation when it came to new inventions. Since he

was poor as a young person, he came in contact with common people and had great sympathy for the various problems they faced, which was why many of his inventions had to do with improving working tools and methods.

His first major invention was an improvement in a particular method of weaving silk that formed a pattern on the surface of the fabric. (In Europe, this weave was much later to become known as jacquard weave.) The looms used in the weaving were crude and hard to use, so that weavers might spend a month painstakingly creating one bolt of cloth. Through careful observation and much thought, Ma Jun discovered that there were many repetitive motions in the coloration and patterning and that these could be simplified by modifying the way the loom was constructed. This greatly increased productivity. The silk fabrics that the Wei emperor Wei Mingdi was later to bestow on foreign emissaries were the product of looms that utilized Ma Jun's improvements.

At one point, Ma Jun served as a low-level official in the Wei capital. One day, he and a number of higher officials were debating on the subject of whether or not there had been a "compass-cart" in ancient days. The officials all felt that references to such a thing in historical records were unreliable, while Ma Jun felt it was quite likely that the ancients had created this device for indicating direction with the use of a magnetized piece of metal. To prove his point about how inventing such a thing was not so difficult, he himself soon made one with the help of craftsman that was not dissimilar to what was referenced in the ancient records. The debate was over when Ma Jun's magnet appeared. People also began to recognize his creative ingenuity.

Ma Jun's most famous invention was a water wheel used in irrigating fields. The two main devices used at the time were called jie gao and lu lu, the first of which used the principle of a lever and the second the principle of a wheel. These two had never been put together in one machine to allow a continuous flow of water, and therefore the efficiency of the existing irrigation devices was quite low. When Ma Jun lived in Luoyang, he discovered that a particular patch of land would be suitable for growing things but since it was on high ground, it needed to be irrigated. He tried to figure out a way to irrigate it that economized on both time and labor. After much thinking and experimentation, he came up with a new invention that was called the "fan che," or a kind of water "tipper" that utilized both principles of leverage and water wheel. A person stood on two lever-boards and alternatively pressed down on them, which transmitted the force to an axle that turned a water-wheel. In this way, a continuous stream of water could be channeled from a lower place to a higher. The mechanisms of this device were so clever and so convenient that even a child could use it and it was greatly welcomed by the populace. It was quickly put into widespread use. Later generations improved upon the device and until the invention of modern pumps it was the most advanced water-lifting device known to man. It can still be seen in use in some places.

Ma Jun dreamed up a number of other inventions but, since rulers at the time did not make good use of his talents, he was not able to realize them. Many people did enjoy the fruits of his labors, though, and they sang his praises.

蒙恬发明毛笔

原文：

tián bǐ lún zhǐ
恬 笔 伦 纸

故事：

用笔头柔软的毛笔在纸上写出线条优美的汉字，是中国文化的一大特点。古代中国人认为，毛笔是由秦朝（前221—前206）时候的将军蒙（méng）恬发明的。

蒙恬的家族世代都担任秦国的将军，到了他这一代，成就更为辉煌。秦始皇任命蒙恬为将军，负责对外的战争；他弟弟也被任命为大臣，负责秦国内部的事务。蒙恬在秦统一六国的战争中立下功劳。当时，秦的边境经常受到游牧民族匈奴军队的掠夺，趁着秦与六国作战的机会，匈奴占领了大片土地，抢走了很多牲畜、财产。秦朝建立后，蒙恬奉命率领几十万大军抗击匈奴。他还负责修筑了万里长城，把匈奴挡在了长城以北的地区。

统一六国之前，蒙括曾率领军队，在属于赵国的中山地区与楚国交战。战争进行期间，蒙恬经常写报告向秦王汇报战场上的情况。开始的时候，他跟其他人一样，用竹签蘸着墨汁，在丝做的绢布上面写字。竹签是硬的，沾不上多少墨汁，写不了几个字就得停下来再蘸一次墨汁；为了防止墨汁滴下来把贵重的绢弄脏，写字的时候要很小心。这样一来，写一份报告就要花很长时间。蒙恬觉得这种笔很不好用，就产生了发明一种新型书写工具的想法。

中山地区有很多野兔，又肥又大，战争的间隙，蒙恬喜欢到野外去猎兔。有一天，他带着猎杀的几只兔子回军营，无意中发现兔子的尾巴上面沾了血液，血水在地上拖出了红色的痕迹。蒙恬灵机一动，是不是可以用兔尾上的毛来写字呢？他马上剪下一束兔尾巴上的毛，把它们插在一根竹管上，试着用它来写字。可是兔毛上面有油，不吸墨汁，看来不适合用来写字。

蒙恬不是那么容易放弃的人，他又开始寻找使兔毛可以吸取墨汁的方法。后来他发现，将兔毛放在含有石灰质的水坑里，兔毛上的油脂就会被去掉，兔毛变得洁白而柔软，可以吸取不少水分。蒙恬将这支新做的笔往墨汁里一蘸，兔毛果然吸

足了墨汁，写起字来很流畅，而且写出的字体也显得圆润漂亮。蒙恬非常高兴，从此，他就开始用这种笔写报告，写得又快又好。

蒙恬发明的毛笔开始用的是兔子的毛，后来，他又尝试用其他动物的毛，发现山羊的毛效果也很好。他的发明传到了其他人那里，又有人尝试把不同的毛混杂在一起使用。这样一来，毛笔的品种就更丰富了。

事实上，出土文物表明，在蒙恬之前很久，中国人就开始使用毛笔了。蒙恬应该是毛笔的改良者，但他所制的毛笔比较好用，所以后人就将他视为毛笔的发明者。

Meng Tian Invents the Brush

Calligraphing Chinese characters on paper with a soft-tipped brush is one of the unique features of Chinese culture. People in ancient times believed that this invention could be attributed to a general named Meng Tian, who lived in the time of the Qin dynasty (221–206 BCE).

Generations of Meng Tian's family served as generals in the state of Qin. By his generation, the accomplishments of the clan were glorious and Qin Shi Huang appointed Meng Tian to be general in charge of foreign wars. His little brother, meanwhile, was appointed a senior Minister in charge of domestic affairs. Meng Tian was notable in helping unify the six other principalities under the rule of the Qin. At the same time, the armies of nomadic tribes would frequently plunder the frontiers of Qin territory and, taking advantage of the Qin, focus on conquering these six nations, would occupy large swathes of land and plunder livestock and possessions. Once the Qin dynasty was established, Meng Tian received the emperor's commission to lead armies in battle against the Hun. He was also charged with rebuilding the Great Wall, to contain the Hun in territories to its north.

Before the unification of the six nations, Meng Tian led armies in war against the state of Chu, on lands in the Zhongshan region that belonged to the state of Zhao. In the course of this war, Meng Tian often had to write progress reports back to the Qin ruler. At the beginning, like everyone else, he wrote on a piece of silk fabric with a sharpened piece of bamboo dipped in ink. The bamboo sliver was stiff and did not absorb ink, so the work of dipping it time and again was tedious, plus one had to be extremely careful not to allow drops of ink to fall on the precious silk. Writing just one report took a long time. Meng

Tian's realization that this way of doing things was unacceptable was what led to the invention of a new writing utensil.

The Zhongshan region contained many big, fat, wild rabbits. In intervals between battles, Meng Tian enjoyed going out hunting and one day he returned to his camp with several rabbits. Blood was dripping off the tail of one of them, and he noticed that it left a red line in the snow. Inspired, he wondered if the fur of the rabbit could be used for writing. He promptly cut fur off the tail, secured it in a bamboo section and used it to write characters. He discovered, however, that the fur contained oil and therefore did not absorb ink.

Not deterred, he began to look for ways to improve the ability of rabbit-fur to absorb ink. He found that soaking the fur in water that contained lime took off the oil and made the fur soft, pure white, and able to absorb much more water. It also absorbed ink, and made the writing of characters not only a fluid and easy process, but one that resulted in lines that could be beautifully calligrapied. Delighted, Meng Tian began to use this kind of brush to write quicker and better reports.

Meng Tian used the fur of a rabbit for his brushes in the beginning. Later he tried using the fur of other animals, and he discovered that the cashmere of cashmere goats was particularly effective. Soon his invention was being adopted by others, who also experimented with combining different kinds of hair for better results. There was soon a

wealth of different types and varieties of brushes.

In point of fact, from excavated artifacts we now know that brushes had been invented by Chinese long before Meng Tian. He can still be praised for having made improvements. It may be that since his brushes were easier to use, people came to attribute the original invention to him.

蔡伦造纸

原文：

tián bǐ lún zhǐ
恬 笔 伦 纸

故事：

造纸术是中国对世界文明作出的极为宝贵的贡献。很难想象，假如没有纸，世界会是什么样子。纸的发明大大促进了文明的传播与交流，深刻影响了世界历史的进程。而提到造纸术，就不能不想到它的发明者蔡伦。

蔡伦是东汉时候的人，少年时期即进入宫廷，担任皇帝的侍从。汉和帝做皇帝时，他被任命为皇室生产作坊的负责人，为皇室提供各种器物。他聪明好学而又认真负责，在他的监督下，皇室生产作坊里出产的器物无论质量、性能还是外观都十分出色。

汉和帝的皇后姓邓，她喜欢读书和写作，但苦于没有轻便的书籍和数量足够的书写材料。当时的书籍和文件大多写在竹简上，极其笨重。皇室和贵族也用丝绸来书写，但因为丝绸产量少、价格昂贵，也不可能大量使用。蔡伦注意到这一问

题，决心寻找一种轻便而又可以大量制造的新材料。

在此之前，已经有人制作出了一些植物纤维纸，但质量不稳定，原料采用麻布，产量也无法提高。蔡伦觉得这是一个发展方向，就到作坊里进行研究和试验。他认真总结前人的经验，觉得首先应该扩大造纸原料的来源，其次是改进造纸的技术，提高纸张质量。他试着用树皮来造纸，因为树皮是容易获得的原料。但是树皮加工起来难度比较大，蔡伦想了各种办法改进造纸技术，终于用树皮制成了质量不错的纸张。蔡伦受到鼓舞，开始试用其他原料，造纸技术也越来越成熟。到最后，他用树皮、碎布、麻头、破旧的鱼网等容易获得的原料都精制出了优质的纸张。

蔡伦把他制造出来的一批优质纸张献给汉和帝和邓皇后，汉和帝十分满意，称赞了他的才能，命令全国都推广蔡伦的造纸术。这样，蔡伦的造纸术很快传遍各地。他继续完善造纸的工艺，制造出了专供皇室使用的高级纸张。对他的发明创造最高兴的是邓皇后，因为有了轻便而数量足够的纸张，她就可以无拘无束地写作了。她还下令抄写了大量典籍，使纸制的书籍迅速增加。

在蔡伦献纸之后，造纸技术和纸张广为流传，纸成为主要的书写材料，中国文化得到很大发展。蔡伦被后人认为是极具科学天赋的古代发明家。

Cai Lun Makes Paper

The invention of paper-making technology is one of China's valuable contributions to the rest of the world. Without paper, it is hard to imagine what the world would be like today, since the invention of paper was of major importance in improving communications and transmitting civilization. It profoundly influenced the advance of human history. One cannot mention paper-making technology without thinking of the inventor named Cai Lun.

Cai Lun lived during the period of Eastern Han. He entered the court as a young man and served as an imperial attendant. When Han Hedi was emperor, Cai was put in charge of the imperial workshops, producing all kinds of articles for the imperial chambers. Cai was industrious and studious, as well as highly responsible, and under his stewardship the imperial workshops produced items of outstanding quality, usefulness, and beauty.

The empress of Han Hedi, named Deng, loved to read but also to write and she regretted not having adequate materials at hand. Books and documents were mainly written on bamboo strips at the time, which were cumbersome. The imperial chambers and the aristocrats also used silk for writing, but since the quantity of silk produced was very small, and the price was high, it could not be used in any wide-spread fashion. Cai Lun took note of this and determined to find a light, convenient, new material that could be produced in quantity.

Before this time, people had already experimented with using different kinds of plant fibers to make paper but the quality was uneven. Since the raw material was mainly hemp cloth, the quantity could also not be greatly increased. Cai Lun felt that using plant fibers was the

direction to pursue, however, so his workshops began experimentation and research. Cai conscientiously gathered data on what people had done already. He felt that the first step was to expand the source of raw materials for paper making, before trying to improve the technology for actual production or to raise paper quality. He tried using bark to make paper, since bark was easily available. Processing bark was relatively difficult, however, so Cai Lun then addressed technical issues and finally came up with paper made from bark that was of acceptable

quality. Encouraged by this, he began to experiment with other materials, and as he worked he became more and more familiar with the technology as well. In the end, he used a whole range of easily available materials to make quite fine papers, including bark, scraps of fabric, cotton bolls, old fish netting and so on.

When Cai Lun presented the finer papers he had made to the emperor Han Hedi and Empress Deng, the emperor was quite pleased and praised his talents and ordered the entire country to promote his paper-making technologies. Cai Lun's techniques were soon propagated throughout the entire land. He continued to improve his paper-making artistry and made high-quality papers that were to be used only in the imperial chambers. The one who was happiest about his inventions was the Empress Deng. With light-weight paper, made in quantity, she was now able to write without constraints. In addition, she ordered that the classics be copied out by others, which rapidly increased the number of books that were written on paper.

After Cai Lun's contributions in the field, paper-making technologies and factories were set up and paper became the primary material for writing, a change that gave strong impetus to the spread and development of Chinese culture. Cai Lun has long been regarded as one of China's ancient inventors who was naturally endowed with great scientific gifts.

《千字文》

tiān dì xuán huáng，yǔ zhòu hóng huāng。
天地玄黄，宇宙洪荒。

rì yuè yíng zè，chén xiù liè zhāng。
日月盈昃，辰宿列张。

hán lái shǔ wǎng，qiū shōu dōng cáng。
寒来暑往，秋收冬藏。

rùn yú chéng suì，lǜ lǚ tiáo yáng。
闰余成岁，律吕调阳。

yún téng zhì yǔ，lù jié wéi shuāng。
云腾致雨，露结为霜。

jīn shēng lì shuǐ，yù chū kūn gāng。
金生丽水，玉出昆冈。

jiàn hào jù què, zhū chēng yè guāng
剑号巨阙，珠称夜光。

guǒ zhēn lǐ nài, cài zhòng jiè jiāng
果珍李柰，菜重芥姜。

hǎi xián hé dàn, lín qián yǔ xiáng
海咸河淡，鳞潜羽翔。

lóng shī huǒ dì, niǎo guān rén huáng
龙师火帝，鸟官人皇。

shǐ zhì wén zì, nǎi fú yī shang
始制文字，乃服衣裳。

tuī wèi ràng guó, yǒu yú táo táng
推位让国，有虞陶唐。

diào mín fá zuì, zhōu fā yīn tāng
吊民伐罪，周发殷汤。

zuò cháo wèn dào, chuí gǒng píng zhāng
坐朝问道，垂拱平章。

ài yù lí shǒu, chén fú róng qiāng
爱育黎首，臣伏戎羌。

xiá ěr yì tǐ, shuài bīn guī wáng
遐迩一体，率宾归王。

míng fèng zài zhú, bái jū shí chǎng
鸣凤在竹，白驹食场。

huà bèi cǎo mù, lài jí wàn fāng
化被草木，赖及万方。

gài cǐ shēn fà, sì dà wǔ cháng
盖此身发，四大五常。

gōng wéi jū yǎng, qǐ gǎn huǐ shāng
恭惟鞠养，岂敢毁伤。

nǚ mù zhēn jié, nán xiào cái liáng
女慕贞洁，男效才良。

zhī guò bì gǎi, dé néng mò wàng
知过必改，得能莫忘。

wǎng tán bǐ duǎn, mǐ shì jǐ cháng
罔谈彼短，靡恃己长。

xìn shǐ kě fù, qì yù nán liáng
信使可覆，器欲难量。

mò bēi sī rǎn，shī zàn gāo yáng
墨悲丝染，《诗》赞羔羊。

jǐng xíng wéi xián，kè niàn zuò shèng
景行维贤，克念作圣。

dé jiàn míng lì，xíng duān biǎo zhèng
德建名立，形端表正。

kōng gǔ chuán shēng，xū táng xí tīng
空谷传声，虚堂习听。

huò yīn è jī，fú yuán shàn qìng
祸因恶积，福缘善庆。

chǐ bì fēi bǎo，cùn yīn shì jìng
尺璧非宝，寸阴是竞。

zī fù shì jūn，yuē yán yǔ jìng
资父事君，曰严与敬。

xiào dāng jié lì，zhōng zé jìn mìng
孝当竭力，忠则尽命。

lín shēn lǚ bó，sù xīng wēn qìng
临深履薄，夙兴温清。

sì lán sī xīn, rú sōng zhī shèng.
似兰斯馨，如松之盛。

chuān liú bù xī, yuān chéng qǔ yìng.
川流不息，渊澄取映。

róng zhǐ ruò sī, yán cí ān dìng.
容止若思，言辞安定。

dǔ chū chéng měi, shèn zhōng yí lìng.
笃初诚美，慎终宜令。

róng yè suǒ jī, jiè shèn wú jìng.
荣业所基，籍甚无竟。

xué yōu dēng shì, shè zhí cóng zhèng.
学优登仕，摄职从政。

cún yǐ gān táng, qù ér yì yǒng.
存以甘棠，去而益咏。

yuè shū guì jiàn, lǐ bié zūn bēi.
乐殊贵贱，礼别尊卑。

shàng hé xià mù, fū chàng fù suí.
上和下睦，夫唱妇随。

wài shòu fù xùn, rù fèng mǔ yí
外受傅训，入奉母仪。

zhū gū bó shū, yóu zǐ bǐ ér
诸姑伯叔，犹子比儿。

kǒng huái xiōng dì, tóng qì lián zhī
孔怀兄弟，同气连枝。

jiāo yǒu tóu fèn, qiē mó zhēn guī
交友投分，切磨箴规。

rén cí yǐn cè, zào cì fú lí
仁慈隐恻，造次弗离。

jié yì lián tuì, diān pèi fěi kuī
节义廉退，颠沛匪亏。

xìng jìng qíng yì, xīn dòng shén pí
性静情逸，心动神疲。

shǒu zhēn zhì mǎn, zhú wù yì yí
守真志满，逐物意移。

jiān chí yǎ cāo, hǎo jué zì mí
坚持雅操，好爵自縻。

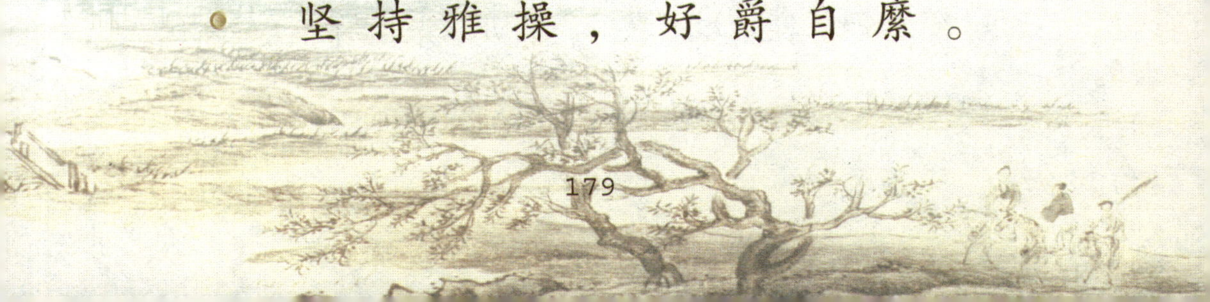

dū yì huá xià，dōng xī èr jīng
都邑华夏，东西二京。

bèi máng miàn luò，fú wèi jù jīng
背邙面洛，浮渭据泾。

gōng diàn pán yù，lóu guàn fēi jīng
宫殿盘郁，楼观飞惊。

tú xiě qín shòu，huà cǎi xiān líng
图写禽兽，画彩仙灵。

bǐng shè bàng qǐ，jiǎ zhàng duì yíng
丙舍傍启，甲帐对楹。

sì yán shè xí，gǔ sè chuī shēng
肆筵设席，鼓瑟吹笙。

shēng jiē nà bì，biàn zhuǎn yí xīng
升阶纳陛，弁转疑星。

yòu tōng guǎng nèi，zuǒ dá chéng míng
右通广内，左达承明。

jì jí fén diǎn，yì jù qún yīng
既集坟典，亦聚群英。

dù gǎo zhōng lì, qī shū bì jīng
杜稿钟隶，漆书壁经。

fǔ luó jiàng xiàng, lù xiá huái qīng
府罗将相，路侠槐卿。

hù fēng bā xiàn, jiā jǐ qiān bīng
户封八县，家给千兵。

gāo guàn péi niǎn, qū gǔ zhèn yīng
高冠陪辇，驱毂振缨。

shì lù chǐ fù, chē jià féi qīng
世禄侈富，车驾肥轻。

cè gōng mào shí, lè bēi kè míng
策功茂实，勒碑刻铭。

pán xī yī yǐn, zuǒ shí ē héng
磻溪伊尹，佐时阿衡。

yǎn zhái qū fù, wēi dàn shú yíng
奄宅曲阜，微旦孰营？

huán gōng kuāng hé, jì ruò fú qīng
桓公匡合，济弱扶倾。

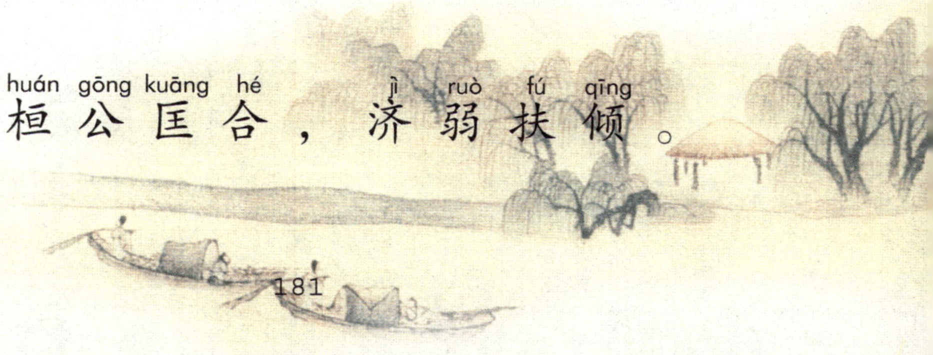

qǐ huí hàn huì，yuè gǎn wǔ dīng。
绮回汉惠，说感武丁。

jùn yì mì wù，duō shì shí níng。
俊乂密勿，多士寔宁。

jìn chǔ gēng bà，zhào wèi kùn héng。
晋楚更霸，赵魏困横。

jiǎ tú miè guó，jiàn tǔ huì méng。
假途灭虢，践土会盟。

hé zūn yuē fǎ，hán bì fán xíng。
何遵约法，韩弊烦刑。

qǐ jiǎn pō mù，yòng jūn zuì jīng。
起翦颇牧，用军最精。

xuān wēi shā mò，chí yù dān qīng。
宣威沙漠，驰誉丹青。

jiǔ zhōu yǔ jì，bǎi jùn qín bìng。
九州禹迹，百郡秦并。

yuè zōng tài dài，shàn zhǔ yún tíng。
岳宗泰岱，禅主云亭。

yàn mén zǐ sài， jī tián chì chéng
雁门紫塞，鸡田赤城。

kūn chí jié shí， jù yě dòng tíng
昆池碣石，巨野洞庭。

kuàng yuǎn mián miǎo， yán xiù yǎo míng
旷远绵邈，岩岫杳冥。

zhì běn yú nóng， wù zī jià sè
治本于农，务兹稼穑。

chù zài nán mǔ， wǒ yì shǔ jì
俶载南亩，我艺黍稷。

shuì shú gòng xīn， quàn shǎng chù zhì
税熟贡新，劝赏黜陟。

mèng kē dūn sù， shǐ yú bǐng zhí
孟轲敦素，史鱼秉直。

shù jī zhōng yōng， láo qiān jǐn chì
庶几中庸，劳谦谨敕。

líng yīn chá lǐ， jiàn mào biàn sè
聆音察理，鉴貌辨色。

yí jué jiā yóu, miǎn qí zhī zhí
贻厥嘉猷，勉其祗植。

xǐng gōng jī jiè, chǒng zēng kàng jí
省躬讥诫，宠增抗极。

dài rǔ jìn chǐ, lín gāo xìng jí
殆辱近耻，林皋幸即。

liǎng shū jiàn jī, jiě zǔ shuí bī
两疏见机，解组谁逼？

suǒ jū xián chǔ, chén mò jì liáo
索居闲处，沉默寂寥。

qiú gǔ xún lùn, sàn lǜ xiāo yáo
求古寻论，散虑逍遥。

xīn zòu lěi qiǎn, qī xiè huān zhāo
欣奏累遣，戚谢欢招。

qú hé dì lì, yuán mǎng chōu tiáo
渠荷的历，园莽抽条。

pí pá wǎn cuì, wú tóng zǎo diāo
枇杷晚翠，梧桐蚤凋。

chén gēn wěi yì，luò yè piāo yáo。
陈根委翳，落叶飘摇。

yóu kūn dú yùn，líng mó jiàng xiāo。
游鹍独运，凌摩绛霄。

dān dú wán shì，yù mù náng xiāng。
耽读玩市，寓目囊箱。

yì yóu yōu wèi，zhǔ ěr yuán qiáng。
易輶攸畏，属耳垣墙。

jù shàn cān fàn，shì kǒu chōng cháng。
具膳餐饭，适口充肠。

bǎo yù pēng zǎi，jī yàn zāo kāng。
饱饫烹宰，饥厌糟糠。

qīn qi gù jiù，lǎo shào yì liáng。
亲戚故旧，老少异粮。

qiè yù jì fǎng，shì jīn wéi fáng。
妾御绩纺，侍巾帷房。

wán shàn yuán jié，yín zhú wěi huáng。
纨扇圆洁，银烛炜煌。

zhòu mián xī mèi, lán sǔn xiàng chuáng
昼眠夕寐，蓝笋象床。

xián gē jiǔ yàn, jiē bēi jǔ shāng
弦歌酒宴，接杯举觞。

jiǎo shǒu dùn zú, yuè yù qiě kāng
矫手顿足，悦豫且康。

dí hòu sì xù, jì sì zhēng cháng
嫡后嗣续，祭祀烝尝。

qǐ sǎng zài bài, sǒng jù kǒng huáng
稽颡再拜，悚惧恐惶。

jiān dié jiǎn yào, gù dá shěn xiáng
笺牒简要，顾答审详。

hái gòu xiǎng yù, zhí rè yuàn liáng
骸垢想浴，执热愿凉。

lǘ luó dú tè, hài yuè chāo xiāng
驴骡犊特，骇跃超骧。

zhū zhǎn zéi dào, bǔ huò pàn wáng
诛斩贼盗，捕获叛亡。

bù shè liáo wán, jī qín ruǎn xiào
布射僚丸，嵇琴阮啸。

tián bǐ lún zhǐ, jūn qiǎo rén diào
恬笔伦纸，钧巧任钓。

shì fēn lì sú, bìng jiē jiā miào
释纷利俗，并皆佳妙。

máo shī shū zī, gōng pín yán xiào
毛施淑姿，工颦妍笑。

nián shǐ měi cuī, xī huī lǎng yào
年矢每催，曦晖朗曜。

xuán jī xuán wò, huì pò huán zhào
璇玑悬斡，晦魄环照。

zhǐ xīn xiū hù, yǒng suí jí shào
指薪修祜，永绥吉劭。

jǔ bù yǐn lǐng, fǔ yǎng láng miào
矩步引领，俯仰廊庙。

shù dài jīn zhuāng, pái huái zhān tiào
束带矜庄，徘徊瞻眺。

gū lòu guǎ wén, yú méng děng qiào
孤陋寡闻，愚蒙等诮。

wèi yǔ zhù zhě, yān zāi hū yě
谓语助者，焉哉乎也。

图书在版编目（CIP）数据

《千字文》故事：汉英对照/姜晓东著；（美）艾梅霞(Avery,M.)译.—北京：五洲传播出版社，2009.12
（中国蒙学经典故事丛书）
ISBN 978-7-5085-1736-0

Ⅰ.①千… Ⅱ.①姜…②艾… Ⅲ.①汉语-对外汉语教学-语言读物 ②汉语-古代-启蒙读物
Ⅳ.①H195.5②H194.1

中国版本图书馆CIP数据核字（2009）第207546号

主　　编：荆孝敏　邓锦辉
副 主 编：王　峰
顾　　问：赵启正　沈锡麟　潘　岳
　　　　　周黎明（美）　李莎（加）　威廉·林赛（英）
监　　制：林武汉
著　　者：姜晓东
翻　　译：艾梅霞（美）
责任编辑：王　峰
设计指导：缪　惟
设计制作：潘宏伟　林国霞
插　　图：李思东

《千字文》故事

出版发行：五洲传播出版社
社　　址：北京市海淀区莲花池东路北小马厂6号华天大厦
邮政编码：100038
电　　话：010-58891281
传　　真：010-58891281
制版单位：北京锦绣圣艺文化发展有限公司
印　　刷：北京彩和坊印刷有限公司
开　　本：787x1092　1/16
印　　张：12.25
版　　次：2010年1月第1版　2010年1月第1次印刷
书　　号：ISBN 978-7-5085-1736-0
定　　价：79.00元